D1527744

DEBT

CHARLOTTE BYRD

DEBT

I owe him a debt. A big one.

A **dark and dangerous** stranger paid for my mother's cancer treatment, saving her life.

Now I owe him. But I can't pay it back with money, not that I even have any.

He wants only one thing: Me.

His for one year.

Will I walk away in one piece?

"Fast-paced, dark, addictive, and compelling" - Amazon Reviewer ★★★★★

"Hot, steamy, and a great storyline." - Christine Reese ★★★★★

"My oh my....Charlotte has made me a fan for life." - JJ, Amazon Reviewer ★★★★★

"The tension and chemistry is at five alarm level." - Sharon, Amazon reviewer ★★★★★

"Hot, sexy, intriguing journey of Elli and Mr. Aiden Black. - Robin Langelier ★★★★★

"Wow. Just wow. Charlotte Byrd leaves me speechless and humble... It definitely kept me on the edge of my seat. Once you pick it up, you won't put it down." - Amazon Review ★★★★★

"Sexy, steamy and captivating!" - Charmaine, Amazon Reviewer ★★★★★

" Intrigue, lust, and great characters...what more could you ask for?!" - Dragonfly Lady ★★★★★

"An awesome book. Extremely entertaining, captivating and interesting sexy read. I could not put it down." - Kim F, Amazon Reviewer ★★★★★

"Just the absolute best story. Everything I like to read about and more. Such a great story I will read again and again. A keeper!!" - Wendy Ballard ★★★★★

"It had the perfect amount of twists and turns. I instantaneously bonded with the heroine and of course Mr. Black. YUM. It's sexy, it's sassy, it's steamy. It's everything." - Khardine Gray, Bestselling Romance Author ★★★★★

CHAPTER 1 - SOPHIA

I enter the double-wide trailer, which has been my home since I was six, with a sense of dread. My mom's hospital bed barely fits into the back room, and ever since we had that installed, everything else had to be moved around and put into every crevice throughout the house it would fit in. Clothes, boxes, shoes, and magazines are everywhere. Now that Mom's not working at the bar, I have to work twice as many hours just to make the same amount of money. And it's never enough.

She has to take more and more pills, and the prices are constantly changing. Last month, one of her pills cost forty dollars for a one-week supply, and now it's $325 for the same amount, without much of an explanation as to why. I empty my pockets. The tips from the regulars after an eight-hour shift are a little over twelve dollars. I don't blame them. They don't have much to spare themselves. But it's not enough. Not nearly enough.

I reach into my other pocket and pull out a crisp one-hundred-dollar bill. I've never received a tip that big before and I'm eternally grateful. It will go a long way to paying for this month's rent. It might even let me get some of my mom's jewelry from that pawn shop. No, I can't think like that. Medication is more important than heirlooms.

"Is that you, Sophia?" I hate how faint my mom's voice is. She used to be such a tough and strong woman. She never took shit from anyone, especially not men. I'm much shyer and unsure of myself than she is. Not as confident. Not as strong. But now, my mom is weak and tired.

"Don't come in yet," she says when I approach the door.

"Mom, it's okay," I say through the door. I hear her moving around in the bed and making a ruckus. Things are falling over and glass shatters.

"Shit, shit, shit," she says. I'm about to open the door.

"Don't you dare open that door, Sophia Elizabeth Cole."

When Mom uses my full name, I know she really means it.

After a couple more minutes, she shouts, "Okay, I'm ready!"

I walk in. She's looking into her compact and adjusting her wig. Her face is made up to the ten. Her eyebrows are penciled in, and she's even wearing fake eyelashes. She finishes off the look with a generous slather of lipstick and smiles at me.

"You look beautiful," I say, trying to hold back tears.

"Oh, c'mon, don't start now. If you cry, you'll make me cry, and then all this work will go to hell."

I smile. I love my mom's soft Southern accent. She was born in Kentucky and moved to California when she was sixteen with her first husband, but her accent never went away.

"What would you like for dinner?" I ask, trying to change the subject. Mom looks like she's ready to go to a ball, but all we will be doing is sitting around the television with tray tables and eating whatever concoction I dream up.

"Macaroni and cheese?" she asks.

"Again?" We've had it for a week straight.

"I'm afraid it's the only thing I can keep down nowadays."

I nod and head to the kitchen. When I get the butter out, tears are flowing out of my eyes uncontrollably and I can't stop them.

Mom worked hard all of her life. She's worked since the age of fourteen, and she deserves better than this. She's only forty-four years old, for goodness sake! And now she's dying a slow and horrible death. She can't eat anything without throwing it up again. The chemo is poisoning her, and we can't even afford the poison anymore. And there's nothing I can do to stop any of this.

———

I COME home and sit by her and I don't know what is worse. My job or my time at home. It's not that I don't want to be here, to spend time with her. It's just that I feel my whole life slipping away along with hers. There was a time when I had dreams. I was a good student. I got A's and B's. I took the SATs. I wanted to go to college. Actually, there was a time when I wanted to go to graduate school. Maybe I could even be a lawyer or a doctor. Something fancy like that. But now? After years of taking care of her and watching her get worse and worse? I don't have much hope for my life anymore.

I sit down next to her and put on an episode of *Grey's Anatomy*. I recently splurged for a Netflix subscription and we have been re-watching this show together ever since. She watches other things when I'm at work, but when I come home, we watch at least two or three episodes of *Grey's*. It's the third season and Dr. Burke's hands aren't working too well. These episodes are scary to me, as I'm sure they are to Mom. What if one of her surgeons is going through something like this? What if his hands aren't working as good as they once were and he's refusing to acknowledge this fact?

I look over at Mom. She looks older than her years. Underneath all the makeup, that is. She has trouble showering and taking care of herself, but one of her favorite things to do is to 'put on her face' as she calls it. Every morning without fail. Her makeup bag sits on the windowsill next to her, within arm's reach. It's all from the local drugstore. None of it is expensive. One of these days, I'd like to take her to Sephora and buy her anything that she wants.

I give her a warm smile and go back to the screen. Dr. Burke's hands are in pain and he makes a mistake in surgery. Blood splatters everywhere. Mom and I exchange glances.

"That's not going to happen to you," I say. "It's just a show."

"I know. Of course, it won't, honey," Mom says with a reassuring smile. She squeezes my hand for good measure. Then I realize that it's not so much that I'm reassuring her, but that she is reassuring me.

"You know, Sophia," Mom says after a moment. "You could be Dr. Burke if you wanted to."

"What?" I ask, taken aback.

"You are still young. You can do anything you want. You are smart and beautiful and competent. And you have your whole life in front of you."

I shrug and look down at the floor.

"I want you to go to college, Sophia. Because that's something you have always wanted to do. I want you to do that, and then I want you to do whatever you want to."

Tears well up in my eyes again.

"What do you want to do, Sophia?"

"I don't know."

"When you were little, you wanted to be a doctor. And when you watched *How to Get Away with Murder,* you wanted to be a lawyer."

"That's the thing. Maybe I just watch too much TV."

"No," she says seriously. "You are a caring, loving

person with a beautiful soul. I just don't want to see you working in that diner for the rest of your life if that's not something you want to do."

"Do you really think I can do something like that?" I ask, pointing to the surgery on TV. "Because that's a bit hard to believe."

"Don't sell yourself short. You have been an amazing caretaker for me. But it's time for you to start being a little less selfish. My time is coming to a close. But your life is just beginning, honey."

I shake my head. "No, no, no," I mumble.

"Yes, I'm sorry."

"You have to keep fighting, Mom."

"I'm tired of fighting, Sophia. Now, I just want to talk about your future. You have done so much for me already, but I just want you to do one more thing."

"What is it?"

"I want you to live your life to the fullest. I want you to go after your dreams."

"But I don't know what my dreams are."

"That's what you'll have to figure out. And once you do, you go after them with all of your strength. Because you deserve to do something that makes you happy, sweetie."

CHAPTER 2 - SOPHIA

WHEN I GET A SURPRISE…

A week later, I am driving home from work on a beautiful, sunny day, thinking that the sky is so blue and there's not a single cloud as far as the eye can see. My legs are cramping up, and I can't wait to get home to climb into bed. I'm not much of a morning person, and these morning shifts are killing me.

I worked from four a.m. until noon, and this eight-hour shift was harder than the busy evening shifts any day. Barely anyone comes in after ten, and breakfast customers don't like to tip as much as dinner customers.

I finally pull onto our street and see the house in the distance. The paint is peeling on the side, and the porch is cluttered with junk, which we no longer have room for inside the house. I need to take care of that one of these days. Just don't know how or when. Paint costs money. Putting junk away doesn't, but I don't know where to put it. A shed is close to one thousand dollars, and I'm not going to have that kind of money anytime soon. Cardboard boxes? Perhaps. But boxes full of junk are easier to steal than loose junk.

The street leading up to the house isn't really a street, but a dirt road. When we first moved here and Mom's second husband, my father, was still around, we would wash the car every week. Within a day, the desert's dry climate and our dirt road would deposit a thin layer of dust on the car, making the exercise fruitless. My father insisted that we had to do it because of pride, but he'd left by the time I turned eight and took the car. I guess his pride extended only to the car, not to his family. We didn't have another car for more than a year after that.

I pull up to the chain-link gate and get out. The neighbor's pit bull and Rottweiler are already going nuts. They welcome me home from work multiple times a day with the excitement of a full marching band and always put a smile on my face.

"Hey, Bella. Boomer." I wave to them. "I'll be right over."

I get back in the car, park, and head over to the dogs. The other neighbors are afraid of them, but they are the sweetest dogs I've ever met. I stick my hands through the chain-link fence and pet them each on their heads.

After the brief hello, which is honestly the highlight of my day, I try to pull the gate closed before heading in. Usually, this is barely a process at all. But today, the wheels on the bottom, which squeak so loudly they send shivers up my spine, get stuck. When I pull them harder, they take off and run over my foot.

"Shit, shit, shit," I curse, hopping on one foot. "Dammit."

The gate needs to be oiled, but I don't really have any extra money to spend on WD-40 or the time to drive out to Home Depot to get it.

"Stupid gate!" I kick it instead. Not a great solution.

I'm about to head inside when, out of the corner of my eye, I see the mail truck. I am about to turn back, but something keeps me here. Getting the mail is not as exciting of an event as it once was. A long time ago, I remembered looking forward to getting cards in the mail from my grandparents and tearing through envelopes with the words "Sweepstakes" and "Winner" on the cover. Nowadays, the only thing that comes in the mail is medical bills.

Despite that, something is holding me back. I wait for the mail truck to pull next to the house. The mailman is a sweet old man who has been delivering mail for close to thirty years or so. Whenever we are short on money, and I have to say that the check is in the mail, even though it isn't, I've always felt bad about it because I know that I'm blaming it on him.

"How's your mom?" he asks. There's no way to really answer that question. Throwing up every morning, afternoon, and night. Staying in bed all day long. People don't want to hear these things.

"Hanging in there," I say. It's the best way to describe the teetering that she's doing between this world and the next.

The mailman hands me a thick stack of envelopes. All are approximately the same size, and I know they're all bills. I sigh and head to the house.

I don't have any money to pay any of the bills. I will have to spend days in the coming week on the phone talking with various administrators at the hospital and Mom's different doctors' offices, all with the hopes of getting some of the bills reduced.

I toss the pile of bills on the kitchen table and open the refrigerator door looking for something to eat. I've been up since 3:30 a.m, so a simple grilled cheese sandwich is a no-brainer. While the skillet is heating up, I check on Mom, who's fast asleep with the blinds still down.

When I sit down at the kitchen table, I reach for the remote to flip on the TV and accidentally knock the stack of bills onto the floor.

"Dammit," I say. I gather all the envelopes, but one stands out. It's different than the rest, and my name is written on it in a beautiful cursive script.

Ms. Sophia Elizabeth Cole

I look at the envelope closer. The paper is fancier than the others, and the stamp is unusual, not the standard issue stamps that they sell at the post office. It has a detailed painting of a buffalo in a field of grass.

There's no return address in the upper left-hand corner. When I turn the envelope around, I see that it's from The Grayson Foundation. Something about that name sounds familiar. Grayson. What's Grayson? Is it Grayson International, the pharmaceutical company?

Instead of tearing the envelope open like I usually do, I get a knife and carefully slice open the top.

DEAR MS. SOPHIA ELIZABETH COLE,

It has come to our attention that your mother is gravely ill. Please use the following check to pay for her treatment.

THERE'S MORE to the letter, but that's the only part I see. I read it over and over, not believing my eyes. I look into the envelope again and pull out a check.

$250,000

CHAPTER 3 - SOPHIA

*T*he check is for a quarter of a million dollars! I don't believe it. This must be fake. A joke. But why? Who would do this? Why would someone play a joke on me like this?

When Mom wakes up, I show her the check and the letter.

"I've seen this on Dr. Phil, Sophia. Don't cash it. It's from some scammer. A love scam."

"But you gotta be talking to someone for them to send you a check like this, don't you?"

"Who have you been talking to?" she asks, furrowing her brows.

"No one! All I do is go to work and take you to doctors' appointments. I don't have any time to waste talking to strangers."

Mom tells me to throw the check away, but I don't listen. Instead, I stay up late after my evening shift and go online. I look up Grayson International. I was right. It's a big pharmaceutical company, which has recently gone public.

The following morning, I look up the Grayson Foundation on my phone and call them. A pleasant young woman answers and confirms that the foundation does indeed exist, and they're located in Los Angeles.

"So are you in the habit of mailing out large checks to strangers?" I ask. I don't mean to be rude or direct, but I don't know how else to go about finding out if this is indeed a real check.

"Ms. Cole, that's primarily all we do," she says.

I'm dumbfounded. I explain my situation to her and wait for her to laugh at me. But she doesn't.

"I can always check your name in our database and make sure that this is a legitimate check that came from us."

"Yes, please, do that."

She asks me to wait on the phone and puts me on hold. I don't wait too long, but the few minutes that do pass feel like it takes a century to expire.

I put on the teapot to pass the time. I also find

one of the last tea bags at the back of the cupboard and make a note to buy more.

"Ms. Cole?" she says. I can barely hear her over the boiling water in the teapot, and I quickly shut it off.

"Yes, I'm here."

"I've got good news for you. Your name is on the list of approved donations, and I also double checked whether a check was actually issued to you, and I see that it was issued five days ago."

I can't respond. I've lost the ability to speak.

"Ms. Cole? Are you there?" she asks. Louder this time.

"Yes, yes, I'm here," I mumble. "So it's okay? I can cash the check?"

"Yes, please do. And if the bank gives you any trouble, just tell them to call this number."

She dictates the number of her boss, and I write it down on the back of the envelope.

When I get off the phone, I don't know if I'm going to cry or laugh. I feel like I could do either. Tears start streaming down my face, and I call for Mom. She's still asleep, but I don't care. We have the money to pay for her treatment. Whatever treatment she needs. My whole body begins to shake, and both my hands and feet go numb.

"Oh my God, Sophia? What's wrong?" Mom comes out of her room and slowly makes her way to me.

"What happened? What's wrong?"

She wraps her arms around me and begins to rock me from side to side. Tears continue to run down my face, but they are not tears of sorrow. I just can't catch my breath long enough to tell her.

"It's going to be okay, baby girl. Whatever it is, we'll get through it."

Suddenly, I start to laugh. "Yes, yes, it is," I say, hugging her back. "It's going to be more than okay, Mom."

"What are you talking about?"

"I just got off the phone with the Grayson Foundation, and the check's legit. They're paying for your treatment. You're going to get some real help now, Mom. And we're going to be okay."

"What are you talking about?" Mom stares at me. I explain, but she just keeps asking me that same question over and over again. Eventually, it sinks in, and I get up and jump around the house, shaking it so hard it feels like it's going to fall over. Mom's too weak to jump around, but she does nod along.

CHAPTER 4 - SOPHIA

WHEN I GO TO CASH THE CHECK...

I drive to the local branch of Bank of America half an hour after I get off the phone with the Grayson Foundation. I can't wait any longer. I'm worried that no matter what they had said on the phone, this isn't going to be real. But some elaborate and very cruel practical joke. From the concerned look on her face, Mom seems to think that, too.

I wait in line behind an elderly gentleman who only starts to take out his wallet when he reaches the glass-plated window. I'm not sure if I can deposit my check here or if I have to wait to meet with one of the higher ups who sit at the desks on the other side of the room and handle home loans and other bigger transactions.

Finally, it's my turn. I walk up to the plexiglass window and hand the teller my check. It's moist from being held in my sweaty hand all this time. I get out my bank card and slide it through.

"Wait...this check is for..." The teller's voice drops off. It's obvious that just like me, this girl has never seen a check for this amount of money before either.

I shrug and nod. She whispers the amount to me as if it were a secret.

"I don't think I can deposit this for you," she says after a moment. My heart drops. What? What is she talking about? She didn't even check if it were okay.

"I'm going to get my manager."

"Okay, thanks," I mumble. My heart is beating so hard it feels like it's about to pop out of my chest.

The manager comes over and looks at the check. Then he looks me up and down. Am I the type of person who is worthy of this amount of money, I imagine him wondering.

"We will need a moment to make sure that everything's in order with this," he finally says.

"Sure, of course." I shrug. I'm giving him permission as if he were asking for it. As I wait, I look up the Grayson Foundation again. Grayson Pharmaceuticals is a big company without any intentions of giving anyone a break on their medication costs. But the Grayson Foundation? Well, their intentions are completely different, at least according to the mission statement on their website. The founder of both is listed as Dr. Grayson, a doctor who developed a particularly effective type of high blood pressure medication and then went into the business of printing money. There are several pictures of him on the website. He is older, but has a kind face. Caring, even. There are pictures of him at the Vanity Fair Oscar Party. And others from a benefit in Palm Springs.

I zoom in on his face. Do I know you? Did I meet you somewhere? At the local drugstore perhaps? Or maybe I served you at the diner? But no matter how hard I look, I draw nothing but a blank.

How else could he have found out about me? Oh, yes, of course! My blog. I started it a while ago. Its purpose was to just document what I've been going through. Initially, I joined a forum for people whose parents are going through cancer. I tended to write these long rambling posts, so after a few weeks, I started posting them on my own blog. I'm not sure what good it did to anyone else, but it helped me. Maybe that's how he found out about me.

"Well, it looks like this check is meant for you,"

the manager says. "We've called the foundation and they did indeed issue you this check."

"I know. That's why I have it."

"Okay, we understand that, Ms. Cole."

I shake my head. On one hand, I can't fault them for checking on this. I mean, who the hell am I to get a check in this amount? But on the other, I hate that they didn't trust me. What have I ever done to not have their trust? I've been nothing but a law-abiding citizen my whole life.

"Okay, so please sign the back and we will put this in your account," the teller says. I do as she says and wait as she feverishly types on her keyboard.

A few moments later, I walk back to my car a quarter of a million dollars richer.

CHAPTER 5 - SOPHIA

*T*wo years ago, I got a check from the Grayson Foundation and twenty months ago, my mom's cancer went into remission. I paid $150,000 for her experimental surgery upfront and they performed it as soon as they flew in the team of specialists from around the country. By the end of the procedure, with the costs of the hospital stay and anesthesiologists and additional post-surgery treatments, there isn't much of that money left. But at least, I have my mom now. Every three months she goes for a checkup, and the more checkups that come and go without a resurgence of cancer, the better her luck is in surviving in the long run.

Every day, I am thankful for that check from that mysterious benefactor. I don't know why we were chosen, but I want more than anything to thank him or her in person. But even that won't do it justice. It's impossible to explain how I really feel about this because it's not just my mom's life that the check saved. It also saved my life.

When Mom was dying, I was living my life day to day, week to week. I made no plans for the future. The future didn't really exist. I barely knew how I was going to get through the week. Now, the future is open and bright.

I even moved out!

I don't live too far now, only a few streets over, but Mom insisted on it.

"A young woman such as yourself needs her own space," she said. "What if you want to bring a guy over? Where are you guys going to hang out? In the living room while I'm snoring in the back room?"

"Mom," I rolled my eyes, "I don't want to bring a guy over."

"Well, I want you to." She looked straight at me. "You're twenty-seven years old now. You've been taking care of me for almost seven years. That's a big burden. You should've been living your own life."

She was right, of course, but I couldn't say that. I didn't regret a moment that I spent caring for her, but a small part of me did wonder how different my life could be.

"Besides." I remember Mom saying. "You need your own place so you can find a guy so you can finally give me grandchildren!"

Grandchildren! I'd been caring for her for so long, I couldn't even imagine having the time in the day to care for children! Let alone, a husband.

And so, with her insistence, I moved out. I got my own trailer a couple of streets away from hers. It's definitely nice to come home to my own place with everything put away neatly in its place. No boxes here. No clothes all over the floor. I have more time to focus on this now. I even have time to focus on other things. Like my future.

My gaze goes to the course catalog laying on my brand-new kitchen table. Well, it's not brand-new; it's from the thrift store down the street, but it's nevertheless my kitchen table. All mine. I leaf through the course catalog. I wonder what else could be mine. Perhaps I could have my own career. A nurse, maybe? I have a lot of experience now. The pay is really good, in comparison to a waitress, anyway. But I don't know if I can care for anyone anymore. Mom's cancer has really worn me out.

"Ding Dong! Ding Dong!" My new doorbell goes off, startling me. Who could that be?

"Yes, may I help you?" I open the door.

There's a mailman at the door. I've never seen him before, so he must be new.

"I have a certified letter here for you, Miss," he says. He doesn't know my name.

"Where's Mr. Thompson? Isn't he still working?"

He looks surprised that I know the other mailman's name.

"Yes, but he's transitioning to an internal role. So I'm going to be filling in for him sometimes."

I nod and sign for the letter.

The envelope looks familiar. The same fancy paper and the same elegant script which had saved Mom's life.

After he pulls away, I turn the envelope over. This time, it's not from the Grayson Foundation. It's from someone named Mr. Francis Whitewater. I open the envelope and take a deep breath. If they're asking for all the money back, I have no way of paying. We've spent it all!

DEAR MS. SOPHIA ELIZABETH COLE,

We have recently learned that your mother has made quite a recovery, and her cancer is now in remission. What great news!

We are pleased that you were able to put the money to such good use, and we are very happy for you.

However, we are now in need of your help. It is my pleasure to invite you to the Grayson House for a brief residency, lasting no longer than a year. We hope you accept the invitation, so that the process of you paying the debt back goes smoothly.

Sincerely,
Mr. Francis Whitewater

CERTAIN WORDS and phrases stand out. I read them over and over again, but they don't make any more sense.

Residency.

No longer than a year.

Debt.

WHAT DOES THAT MEAN?

What is he talking about?

What debt?

"WELL, you didn't think you got that money for nothing, did you?" Dottie asks when I show her the letter at work.

She's close to ninety years old, and she's the only one who I trusted enough to tell about the check. I didn't even tell her anything until after half the money was spent and Mom was on her way to recovery.

"I don't know." I shake my head. "I guess I did."

Dottie laughs. "I've seen a lot in my long life, but this is a new one for me."

"What should I do?"

"I don't know what to do, child." She shakes her head. "But from the looks of this, the letter doesn't seem menacing at all. Maybe they just want you to work there until you pay off your debt."

"Work there? Where?"

"At the Grayson House. Whatever the hell that is."

"But I didn't even know this was a debt. Don't they have the obligation to tell me? Shouldn't I have signed for something if it was going to be a debt?"

"Perhaps, but I don't think this is any normal

kind of debt. This isn't the bank. They would've never given you the money."

I know she's right, of course. No one gave us any money when we needed it. They all turned their backs on us.

"Well, do you think it's something sinister? Like some sort of brothel? Or prostitution ring?" I ask.

I don't know why my mind went there, except that I watch a lot of crime investigation shows on my days off.

Dottie thinks about it for a moment.

"I doubt it," she finally says.

"Those kind of places usually promise you lots of money first and then use you up and toss you out. These people gave you a quarter of a million dollars first without even getting you to sign anything for it."

"And since I didn't sign anything for it, I technically don't have to do anything they say," I say. I feel my eyes lighting up with excitement.

"Well, technically, no," Dottie nods, "but I wouldn't want to play with Karma like that, honey. That might bring a whole lot of bad luck on you."

She's right, of course. I have to go. I owe a debt, and if there is some reasonable and honest way that I can pay it back, then I owe it to them to try.

CHAPTER 6 - SOPHIA

*W*ithin a week of receiving the letter, I quit my job. I had worked there even after we got the money since the money was technically for my mom's treatment. But this time, I quit for good. I don't know when I will be back and I don't want to leave them hanging.

Before I quit, I called Grayson House and spoke to Mr. Francis Whitewater, who came off quite polite and well spoken. He said that my duties at the Grayson House would consist of acting as a personal assistant, answering emails and phone calls, and maybe participating in light cleaning and nursing. When I asked about the nursing aspect, he was very brief and practically refused to give out details, but said that someone had to be taken care of, but the nursing duties are mild. Nothing like the ones I had to perform for my mother.

After I had agreed on the phone to go he sent me an email with the work contract, which I had to sign and return before I could go. I read through the contract carefully and was surprised to learn that I was actually going to get paid for this job. Four times more money than I made at the cafe, and I would also be provided with a one bedroom apartment in which to live on the property.

After all the details were ironed out, I finally told Mom what I was going to do. I didn't tell her about the initial letter, but I did say that I got a new job and it was more than five hours away from her, somewhere in central California. Without missing a beat, she wrapped her arms around me and gave me a warm and encouraging hug.

"I'm so, so happy for you, Sophia," she whispered into my ear, her voice cracking. "I'm so happy that you're finally starting your life out. Going somewhere new. I will definitely come visit you soon!"

Come visit me? I have no idea if this is allowed, or proper or acceptable. I don't know anything about this place, but I agreed.

"Yes, that will be great."

I still have a few months until then to figure things out.

———

TO GET to the Grayson House, I had to take a plane to Chino, California, then a car. I was planning on driving, but Mr. Whitewater insisted that I did not need a car there. I didn't believe him, of course. There's no place in California that doesn't require a car, except maybe the city of San Francisco, but I eventually and reluctantly agreed. Mom and I have only one car, and we share it. I can't take it away from her.

In the baggage claim area of the small local airport, I meet my driver. Desert mountains rise on either side of us near the horizon. This isn't an unfamiliar sight. I'm used to the nature that far-flung places in the wilds of California have to offer.

During the drive, I try to talk to the driver, but he offers very little in the way of information.

"I don't know, miss. You'll find out when you get there," he says over and over again. That's his canned response to almost every question I have about this whole experience.

We turn off the main highway and onto a lonely

desert road. My heart starts to pound and matches the bumps in the road that we drive over. The car isn't your typical sedan. It's a tall Jeep, which is meant for off-road. Just as I thought that the road couldn't be any more off-road, we turn onto an actual off-road road. There are no signs, but the driver turns to the left at the sandy fork in the road. Now we're driving through the desert. Across its wide expanse and over little shrubs and around tall creosote bushes that dot the area.

Finally, somewhere in the distance, I see a large house. It's actually in the middle of nowhere. As we get closer, I make out the beautiful tall white columns that give it grandeur and stature. There are two large white lion statues at the gate. The driver pulls to the intercom and pushes the button.

"We're here," he says. The wrought-iron gates open and let us in. The lions don't move, but continue to stare somewhere into the distance, probably wondering the same thing that I am at this moment: how the hell did we get here?

The driveway is expansive and circular, and the driver pulls up right to the steps of the mansion. I've never been to the White House, but this house looks just like it. The columns are a pristine ivory color.

How the hell they keep them so white in the middle of this dusty desert is beyond me.

"Go on up," the driver says when he comes around and opens my door.

"What about you?" I ask. I don't know him, but I don't want him to leave. I have no idea what awaits me inside. I look at my phone and see that I don't even have one bar. There's absolutely no reception here.

"Oh, I'm not going in there, miss."

There? Why did he say it like that? My heart starts to pound harder. It's so loud, I can barely hear my own thoughts in my head.

The driver gets my two modest suitcases out of the trunk and takes them up the few steps to the porch. The porch is made of beautiful polished wooden slats, and it seems to wrap all the way around the building.

There are two imposing double doors before me. The driver picks up the large metal door knocker and slams it into the door. After two knocks, the door finally opens.

CHAPTER 7 - SOPHIA

WHEN I ARRIVE…

"Ms. Sophia Cole," a small older gentleman says. He's dressed up like a butler from Downtown Abbey.

"My name is Mr. Francis Whitewater, it's my pleasure to meet you."

I shake his extended hand.

"May I help you with your bags?"

I nod, leave one bag on the porch, and go inside with the other one.

"Let me show you to your room," he says, walking past me.

When I enter the lobby, my mouth drops open. The ceilings are close to twenty feet high and gorgeous natural light permeates the space. The desert sun is rather harsh outside, but in here the temperature is a cool and comfortable seventy-five degrees without a whiff of central air. There's a beautiful round marble entry table with a bouquet of flowers in the middle of the entry room the size of a ballroom and two winding staircases frame the table on either side, leading up to the second floor.

"What a beautiful...house?" I say. House doesn't seem like the right word. Mansion? Castle?

"Thank you. I'll let Mr. Grayson know that you approve."

"So, Mr. Grayson? Is that who requested my presence here?" I take the opportunity to ask.

"Yes, of course. I thought that was clear from the letter."

"No." I shake my head. "The letter wasn't very clear about much. The thing is, Mr. Whitewater, I don't even know who Mr. Grayson is. I have no idea why he wants me here. Or what he expects me to do."

Mr. Whitewater turns to face me. "I'm not sure what you're trying to insinuate by that, Ms. Cole, but you are not expected to do anything that you are not 100% willing and interested in doing. Mr. Grayson invited you here as a guest. There is nothing sinister about his intentions."

I nod politely. I'm trying to understand, but rich people have a way of saying things that don't make sense. Supposedly, I'm only here as a guest, but the letter was also quite clear about a certain debt that had to be paid. So what would happen if I didn't pay it?

Mr. Whitewater leads me through the foyer, the gigantic living room with even taller windows, which look out to the expanse of the desert in the background. The windows are so large, floor-to-ceiling, and clear that I feel like I am walking outside.

"You probably have some problems with birds here," I say. I don't know why I bring this up, but large floor-to-ceiling windows always make me wonder about birds.

"How do you mean?" Mr. Whitewater asks with a grave expression of concern on his face.

Now, I'm totally regretting bringing anything up at all. Me and my stupid mouth!

"Well, it's just that the windows are so big and crystal clear..."

He stares at me, waiting for me to continue.

"I just think that you probably have a lot of birds flying into it."

Mr. Whitewater takes a moment to consider the

situation. "You know, come to think of it, yes, we do. It's almost every morning or so that I find one or two dead birds lying on the back porch."

"Oh, how sad," I say. "Well, I guess that's something I can try to fix."

Mr. Whitewater smiles at me. "Perhaps, perhaps."

"You don't think so?" I ask. I'm usually quite good at reading people. Waitressing for seven years has taught me that, if nothing else, but I find Mr. Whitewater difficult to read and analyze. Perhaps, it's his English accent that's throwing me off.

"No, not at all. I just wasn't sure that would be part of your job description."

"I'm not sure either, but I was told that I am here to be a personal assistant and caregiver of the place. Perhaps, within the scope of those duties, I can make some time to try to prevent the deaths of one or two birds per day."

I don't mean to be smug and condescending, but as soon as these words come out of my mouth, I realize that I am. Luckily, Mr. Whitewater lets it slide.

I follow him to the left wing of the house, past the kitchen the size of three doublewide trailers, without another word.

"Well, here we are." Mr. Whitewater reaches into his pocket and gets a keycard. He slides it into an opening on the card reader and then hands it to me.

"This is your room. And this is your card."

We walk into a spacious one-bedroom suite with a full entryway leading to the living room and a large bedroom. The living room and bedroom are separated by French doors and there's also another pair of French doors leading to the private patio outside of the bedroom.

"Wow, this is beautiful."

Mr. Whitewater puts down my bag.

"I'm glad that it's to your liking."

"Yes, definitely. Thank you."

Mr. Whitewater starts to leave, but turns around.

"Oh, yes, I almost forgot. Mr. Grayson is expecting you for dinner at six p.m. There are dresses and shoes in the closet. Jewelry is on the vanity. And you are, of course, welcome to wear your own clothes as well."

I nod, but he doesn't let me off the hook that easily.

"Can I tell him that you are coming?"

"Yes, of course," I mumble.

Of course, I know that I'm supposed to meet this Mr. Grayson at some point. I just didn't think it would be so soon. No, not so soon. It's not soon. It's in a few hours, and I thought I'd meet him right away. I just didn't think that it would be so formal. Dinner? Why doesn't he just come up here? Or I could go to his office? I don't know if I can manage a whole dinner.

After Mr. Whitewater excuses himself, I open the closet. The closet is almost as big as the bedroom.

I've seen these closets before. Walk-in closet with shelves lining all three walls and a large island in the middle. On elegant, real wooden hangers, I find five dresses. Pink, red, black, blue, and green. Each one is more beautiful than the others. One is knee-length made of chiffon. One is short and tight with built-in bra cups. I run my fingers over the dresses and inhale the luxury.

Below the dresses, I find ten pair of different kinds of shoes. All pristine, never worn, without one scuffed up bottom. The heels vary in size, and I quickly try on each one. The flats are the most comfortable, but the high heeled five inch heels with red bottoms make me feel most like a woman.

"Oh my God! What am I doing here?" I say out loud, walking out of the walk-in closet. "People don't do this for nothing. Why does he want me here? To live here?"

Crazy, anti-social thoughts flood my mind. He wants something from me, and whatever he wants isn't easy to get. But what? I shake my head. I don't know.

But then I sit down at the vanity. I slowly open the jewelry box and run my fingers over the pearls. Diamonds glisten and blind me for a moment. But then something else altogether catches my eye. A small pair of elegant silver earrings in the shape of a leaf. And right next to them is another pair. In gold. Yes, this is what I'm going to wear. I don't know which ones, but it's going to be one of these for sure.

I sit on the couch and put my feet up on the soft upholstered coffee table. I need to decide what to do. Hours crawl by, but I am still at an impasse. Finally close to five forty-five, I decide that I will go downstairs and find out what this is all about. I'm a guest here, at least so far, and I will act like a guest. But I won't do anything that I don't feel comfortable with.

I look at the dresses hanging in the closet. They are beautiful, of course, but I'm not a charity case. I don't know who this man is, and I need to retain some power in this relationship. I open my suitcase and look for the best thing that I have. Jeans are too casual. Besides, I don't really have any without any holes in them. T-shirts are also too casual. Aha! A button-down shirt and a pair of khakis. Practical. Professional. Not too sexy. Not sexy at all, actually.

CHAPTER 8 - SOPHIA

I still have some time to kill before dinner. There is no television in the room. A part of me is relieved, yet another is horrified. My phone doesn't work and, though I brought my laptop, there is also no internet connection to be found. What the hell do people do here? I wish that I'd brought some paperbacks from home. My mom has an extensive collection of romance books, and a handful of those would at least keep me entertained in the evenings.

I walk over to the window. The sun is setting and hugging the whole world outside with a warm, comforting hue. This is the color of possibility. Nothing can go wrong in a world bathed in this color. I feel like that's true, but I'm afraid it's not. I look out of the window and see horses grazing in the distance. There's no grass to speak of, but hay is scattered for them on the ground, and they stand with steadfast calmness, which puts me at ease.

I've never ridden a horse, but I've always wanted to. There were only a couple of girls from my high school who rode horses, and both of their families were quite wealthy and owned many acres of ranch land. I always found the idea of living on a ranch very romantic, but now that I am on one, I am not so sure. The idea of Mr. Grayson freaks me out. What kind of elusive and crazy millionaire would ask a stranger to come and live and work in his house for a year? What does he want from me? My mind immediately goes somewhere dark and scary, and I can't let it wander too much. Too much thinking, too many scary thoughts, are not good. Especially since I have to be here for some time.

On the other hand, my mind continues wandering without my permission, this isn't mandatory. Of course, he could keep me here without my permission, but I have no indication that it's what he means to do. So far, everyone has been nothing but nice and professional. Maybe there's nothing sinister about this place at all.

I look at the clock again. I have ten minutes until

dinner. Most girls would need more time, but I don't. I slowly change into my khakis and a pink button down shirt. Something about the pink shirt makes it clash with the khakis, so I try on the blue polka dot button down shirt.

"Yes, this looks much better," I say out loud into the mirror. There's no one around. I'm not used to having so much privacy, given that I grew up in a double-wide with my mom. I'm kind of enjoying the space and the solitude.

"This looks great," I say to myself. I take out my hair tie and flip my head over. When I bring my head back up, my hair falls with much more volume than before. Though it's usually as straight as straw, today it's all in waves around my face.

"Not bad." I smile and run my fingers through it. "Not bad at all."

Makeup. The heat from the long ride from the airport has all but melted off whatever little amount of eyeliner and mascara I'd applied earlier this morning.

I apply a generous amount of eyeliner with my mouth open. I'm not sure what opening my mouth does for eyeliner application, but it's been a habit since I was thirteen. I've also seen girls do it on television, so it must be how it's done.

When all of my makeup, hair, and clothes are done, I again look in the mirror and then at the clock. I still have nine minutes left. How's that possible? Should I go down early? No, I decide. I can't go down early.

My eyes drift back to the closet. I open it again and look at the dresses. I run my fingers over the different fabrics. Each is different from the next. All are much more expensive than any fabric I've ever owned.

I start to unbutton my shirt and pull off my pants before I even realize what I'm doing. Suddenly, I'm pulling on the dress with the thick taffeta skirt on the bottom. The dress poofs out at my hips, and I love how small it makes my legs and waist look.

"Amazing."

I twirl and the dress continues without me. I try on the pair of high heels that are placed right underneath the dress. I've never heard of the company, but I love how pointy the front is and how high the heels are.

I twirl again in front of the window.

I feel like I'm a princess. The fabric feels amazing next to my skin. The taffeta skirt hides my hips and emphasizes my breasts. The polka dots make me feel young, friendly, and alive.

I look back at the clock. I still have a few minutes before dinner if I want to change.

"You should change," I say to myself in the mirror, but the girl who looks back at me doesn't want to.

"If I don't ever see Mr. Grayson again, if I leave tonight after dinner, then at least I got to wear this beautiful dress once." I reason.

I'm rationalizing. Justifying. Trying to give myself reasons to wear it. But I don't need to. I want to wear it. That should be enough.

"Okay." I look in the mirror. "Okay, this is it." I complete the outfit with delicate leaf earrings in silver.

CHAPTER 9 - SOPHIA

WHEN I MEET MR. GRAYSON…

I walk down the elaborate and ornate staircase in my taffeta polka dot dress and high heels. I touch his earrings with my fingertips and shivers run up my spine. My steps are cautious and deliberate. All I hear is the sound my shoes make when they hit the marble and echo off the walls. The walls are lined with beautiful ornate rugs I've only seen in expensive stores on Rodeo Drive. The stairs are a little slippery, and I hold on to the railing. Why they don't put some of those rugs on the staircase is beyond me.

I remember where the kitchen is, and I see Mr. Whitewater in the distance. Near the dining room. I take a deep breath and nearly float the rest of the way over.

"Ms. Sophia Cole, thank you for coming," Mr. Whitewater says to me. He's holding a tray and one tall glass with something in it.

"Would you care for some champagne with strawberries?"

I nod, and he hands me the glass.

"Mr. Grayson is waiting for you in the library."

Library? I wasn't shown a library before. My heart skips a beat. I'm not sure who I'm more excited to see, Mr. Grayson or the library. The presence of a library solves the entire problem of what the hell I'm going to do in my room when I'm not working.

Mr. Whitewater takes me down a hallway which was not part of today's tour. In the end, he turns off to the right into a large spacious room entirely covered in books. Books line every imaginable part of it, from floor to ceiling. The ceiling is about twenty feet, just like in the rest of the house. What really makes the place special is the large bay window overlooking an orange grove.

There's a man sitting there in the shadows. I can't see his face, but I can see his well fitted suit and handsome profile. His hair is brushed back and his nose reminds me of a Roman emperor.

"Mr. Grayson. May I present Ms. Sophia Elizabeth Cole," Mr. Whitewater announces.

I've never been presented before. I don't know what to do. Mr. Grayson gets up and approaches me. His walk is deliberate and considerate. His shoes are so shiny they are bouncing light into my eyes even though it's relatively dark in the library. So dark, in fact, that I can barely make out his face.

"Ms. Sophia Cole," Mr. Grayson says. Immediately, his voice sounds incredibly familiar, but I can't place it. Do I know him? How in the world would I know him?

Finally, Mr. Grayson steps into the light and I see his face.

It's him!

No, it can't be! Can it?

My mouth runs dry. I can't speak.

It's the guy from the cafe. The one who drives the Bentley. The one who asked me out twice.

"It's very nice of you to join me," Mr. Grayson says, extending his hand.

CHAPTER 10 - JAX

*T*wo years earlier...

I am not a particularly complicated man. I like to have fun and lots of it. I have my friends and I have my girls. Not any one girl in particular, of course. More like a revolving door. They come and go and don't stick around for long. And that's what I like about them. Watching them walk away.

It's rare for all of us to get away for a weekend and not go to Vegas, but Logan had been all on us to do something fun that doesn't involve drinking. We're brothers after all, though probably not as close as we should be. We don't get together very often despite the fact that we enjoy pretty much the same things in life - drinking, partying, women. The armchair psychologist in me would say that we're the way we are because of our parents. But who isn't, right? It's amazing that any of us, no matter how good the childhood, emerge unscathed. My brothers and sister and I are lucky. Almost too lucky. Our dad made his money when we were young and we grew up in the lap of luxury. Fancy houses. Fancy cars. Servants. Ability to travel wherever we wanted to at a moment's notice. But all that money...what does it buy exactly, beyond your heart's desires? It doesn't buy a dad who isn't perpetually disappointed. It doesn't buy a mom who is plugged into our lives.

Agh, fuck that. No one wants to hear about some poor little rich boy who has everything in the world and is still unhappy. Still lost.

Lost? Did I just say that? Hell, no. Not me. I'm a playboy. I like to party and I like to hook up with girls. The more the better. That's it. That's all there is to me, as far as my parents are concerned.

So, that's how I find myself here. In the middle of the desert, climbing a boulder the size of a small building. I moan and complain, but if pressed, I'd have to admit the truth. This is fun. Staying up until four a.m., cruising down the Vegas Strip with the perpetual smell of stale cigarette smoke on my clothes does get old. Sometimes.

Hanging off a boulder with one hand, and pulling my whole body to the top has its challenges, but it's also exhilarating as hell. Every muscle in my body is tense as I hang on by just my fingertips.

"You're a natural!" Austin yells from the top. "You can do it."

These are unlikely compliments coming from my eldest brother. But then again, this little climbing trip was all his idea. He's the one who loves the outdoors. He's the one who seems to be looking for answers to all our problems here.

"Thanks," I mumble, finally getting to the top. My other brothers, Logan and Carter, aren't too far behind. Carter is an actor, trying hard to put our family money behind him and make his own. Logan...I'm not entirely sure what he's doing to stay busy nowadays. None of us are Austin though. He's following my dad in the family business. He's the apple of his eye, and by that I mean that the great Dr. Grayson only somewhat approves.

AFTER SPENDING THE MORNING CLIMBING, we leave Joshua Tree National Park and stop by the only decent looking diner on the way out of town. It's small and dusty, full of truck drivers and locals. We stand out like sore thumbs. That's when I see her.

She isn't my type. Not at all. A little plump with messy brown hair and a sweaty forehead from taking too many orders and delivering food to strangers who leave her fifty cent tips. But I want to fuck her right here on the spot.

She is dressed in a plain white T-shirt and ratty jeans. The jeans drag a bit on the floor and the holes are definitely not made by a manufacturer. No respectable girl I know would ever wear something like that, and that makes me want her even more.

Her jeans are tight at the waist, and she adjusts them periodically. Pulling them up over her hips while pulling down her shirt. She is trying to hide her figure, as if she is embarrassed by her gorgeous thighs, hips, and breasts. Contemporary society is all fucked up. This girl's, this woman's, body is what every man with blood running through his veins wants. Every straight man of every race, ethnicity, and creed. A nice waist, shapely hips and legs, and breasts big enough to grab onto. Despite that, all the women's magazines try to do is to convince them that they're too fat because they're not shaped like twelve-year-old boys.

The name tag on her shirt says 'Sophia,' which is

a fancy name to have for a girl who works at a crappy roadside diner. It doesn't take a genius to figure out that this is her full-time job. I would be surprised if she works here to get through school. There isn't an institution of higher learning for a hundred miles in any direction.

No, this Sophia is all wrong for me.

And the worst part? She doesn't have any money.

The thing is that I don't like girls without money. Hear me out. It's not because I'm shallow. It's because I'm practical. I don't fuck girls without money because it gets too complicated. It's much more likely to make things more complicated. Girls without money feel taken advantage of. They want to see me more. They think that a one-night stand is unreasonable, and if it goes past one or two nights then they want me to save them. Rescue them from their pathetic little lives - their words not mine. But I'm not a prince. I'm not a white knight. This isn't the eighteenth century. I don't have it in me, even though I do own a white horse that I love to ride.

I don't like to rescue girls. I don't like needy girls. No, the girls I fuck have to have their own careers – a starring role in a TV show, a signed contract with a leading modeling agency, or at the very least, a reasonably-sized trust fund with one or two million from mommy and daddy. Oh, hell, who are we kidding? It's always from daddy.

I established these rules long ago, and I abide by them religiously. They are there to keep both of us safe. To make sure that we both have fun, but not too much. I don't want the girls I fuck to have expectations of me. If my father taught me anything, it is that I don't live up to expectations.

And now, walking into this cafe and seeing Sophia, I'm ready to toss all of these rules out of the window. I want her. I want to thrust myself deep inside of her and pull her hair until she moans.

I get hard just watching her take an order from an old trucker at the next table.

"Hey, what the hell do you think you're doing?" Sophia says, pushing his hand away from her ass.

I was too focused on her breasts and I hadn't even noticed the trucker's itchy hand reach out and grab her behind.

"Oh, I'm so sorry," he says sarcastically and laughs to his friend.

"Not as sorry as you're going to be," she says, grabbing his uneaten plate of food.

"What are you doing?"

"You can't just go around touching women without permission. Get the hell out."

"Fuck you."

"Get the hell out," she repeats herself calmly.

"But I'm not done eating." The trucker stands up. He reaches for his plate, but she moves it away from him.

"Yes, you are," she says, sending goose bumps down my arms. "Leave or I'm going to call the police."

"For what?"

"For grabbing my ass. That's assault and I'm not putting up with it."

"Assault? Are you kidding?"

"You think you can just touch someone's body without their permission?"

"Yes, I do. What are you going to do about it?" he says, towering over her. Threatening her. His hairy arms are covered in fading tattoos. Just as I'm about to stand up and confront him, Sophia steps forward.

"Then how about this?" she says, grabbing him by the genitals. She squeezes so tight that his whole face gets a sad, sour expression on it. His knees buckle and he sinks a foot below her.

"I'm sorry," he mumbles, raising his hands.

"Now, are you going to leave or should we wait for the cops?" she says, squeezing again.

"Agh!" he yelps in pain. "I'm going to go. I'm sorry."

She lets go and color returns to his face.

"I'd like to see your manager, you little cunt," the trucker hisses, adjusting his dirty hat. "You're going to get fired."

"I'm the manager here. Now get the fuck out!"

I get out of the booth and stand next to her.

"You heard her, sir," I say. "The lady would like you to leave. So, please leave."

People at the nearby booths start to clap and cheer, and my friends join in. The trucker and his friend curse her out one last time, but head toward the door.

"You're a real bitch. You know that? We're never eating here again."

CHAPTER 11 - SOPHIA

WHEN I'M FLUSTERED…

I'm standing right next to her and, though she's trying to stay strong, I can see that she's really shaken. Her chest is flushed, and the trucker's plate is rattling slightly in her hand.

"That was really impressive," I say.

She turns to me.

"I'm probably going to get fired over it."

"I thought you were the manager?"

"No." She shakes her head and starts to gather the plates and cutlery from the trucker's booth. "The manager's coming in later tonight. I'm just the waitress."

"Well, I don't see why you'd get fired. He had no right to grab your ass like that. He was a real asshole."

"Thanks." She smiles. Her smile lights up the room. "Can I get that in writing from you?"

"Yes, of course."

I startle her. Catch her off-guard in a good way. I like that.

"I'm just kidding," she finally says. "Let me just get all this stuff to the kitchen, and I'll come back and take your order."

When I return to the booth, the guys laugh and slap me on the shoulders. They know she's not my type; they know that I'm breaking my rules.

"I don't know, Austin. Looks like Jax's in love." Carter laughs.

"With a waitress!" Austin chimes in.

"What happened to only dating girls with jobs or rich girls? Preferably both?" Logan asks.

"She's got a job," I say. "We're at her job."

"Oh, please. A waitress? That's not a real job. You're breaking your rules, and you know it," Carter jokes.

It's all in good fun, but right now I hate their teasing. They're right of course, and still I want her.

"Nothing's happening. I don't know what you're talking about," I say as assertively as possible.

"We see the way you're looking at her," Logan says. "We're not blind."

"I was just impressed with what she did. Sophia's got spunk."

"Oh, Sophia, is it? You two are on a first name basis already?" Austin chuckles. Dammit. I shouldn't have let that slip.

"It's on her fuckin' name tag, idiot." I try to save myself. But they're not buying it.

Sophia comes back to our table to take our order. After writing down everyone else's orders, she looks up at me from her notepad. I get hard again, and I press on my crotch to keep things at bay.

"You know, you made quite an impression on our brother, Jax here," Carter suddenly says.

"Is that so?"

"I really liked how you handled that trucker," I say. I feel like I'm on my back foot. I don't like coming on to girls in this manner. I glare at Carter, but he doesn't stop.

"Jax was just telling us that you're not at all like the girls we're used to," Carter continues.

"Well, working for a living would do that to you," she says with a smile. I hate how she mocks me for having money. I want her even more now. I want to push her down on the bed, and I want her to let me tie her hands to the bedpost. I want to tease her until she screams my name.

"So what would you like? Jax, is it?" She turns to me.

I had picked out something on the menu, but now I can't remember what it was.

"What would you recommend, Sophia?" I say, reading her name tag. Her name is burned into my brain, but I can't let her know that. Not yet.

"Our spinach omelet with feta cheese is quite good."

"Okay, I'll take that."

———

THE CAFE CLEARS OUT A BIT. While my brothers continue to pick at their food, I excuse myself and head toward the bathroom. Before I get there, I pop into the back and find Sophia sitting on a crate reading a book. She quickly puts it away, but not before I catch the title. *Jane Eyre*. My old English teacher's favorite.

"Can I help you with something?"

"No, not really."

She stares at me. I know I need a reason for being here.

"Yes, actually. I was just wondering if I can take you out for a drink sometime."

I catch her off-guard. Her face lights up, and a brief smile crosses her face.

"That's probably not a good idea," she says with a forlorn sigh.

"Why's that?"

"Well, for one thing, you don't even live here."

"How do you know?" I ask.

She furrows her brows and folds her arms across her chest, pressing her breasts together in front of me. They look as if they are on a platter, and it requires all the strength within me not to reach out and touch them.

"People who drive Bentleys don't live around here."

She's right, of course.

"And the other thing?"

She takes a deep breath.

"I'm not looking for a relationship."

"Who said anything about a relationship?" I ask and immediately regret my choice of words.

"And I'm definitely not looking for anything casual."

"Why's that?" I ask.

I should just drop it, but I can't. No one, and I mean *no one*, has ever turned me down. I can't even believe that this is really happening. Maybe she's just toying with me. Maybe she's just flirting.

"Because I'm not into one-night stands, Jax," she says and walks away. I love the sound of my name in her mouth. I want to put more of me there.

Sophia avoids eye contact with me the rest of the time that we are here. That makes me want her even more. She is feisty and hot, and she doesn't take shit from anyone. An unusual girl. I want her so much, I think I am going to explode.

When she comes over with the check, I purposely extend my hand. She tries to place the plastic cover with the check into my hand, but I take the opportunity to reach out and touch her. Her touch is electric. It sends shivers through my body.

Suddenly, Sophia lets go of the plastic cover, and it drops to the floor.

"I'm sorry," she says. "I'm so clumsy."

"No, I'm the one who's sorry," I apologize.

I see Carter, Austin, and Logan smirking at me from around the table, but my eyes remain fixed on Sophia. When she bends over, her cleavage expands, and her breasts look like they are going to spill out of her T-shirt.

"Thank you," I say and hand Carter the check.

It is Carter's turn to cover the bill. We never split

the bill, unless it is a VIP table at a Vegas nightclub or something extravagant like that. The bill at this roadside café hardly registers as real money.

I make sure that I am the last one out of the booth and quickly slip a one hundred dollar bill under the check.

CHAPTER 12 - SOPHIA

I notice him just as he pulls into our little dusty parking lot with his Bentley. That car costs more money than I'll make in a decade. There are five guys in it, all equally attractive and cocky, but he is the only one who catches my attention.

Tall, handsome, tan. Blue eyes and dark sandy hair that made him look like a brooding dark stranger and a surfer boy, depending on the light.

He strolls into my cafe with a confident and laid back swagger that would make male models jealous. There's a carefree nature to his demeanor and yet, at the same time, there's something very intense about him.

I like the way that he says my name. I like the way

that he's impressed with my ability to deal with
annoying, pestering old men. What he doesn't know
is that, unfortunately, I'm used to unwanted sexual
advances from gross strangers. What that trucker did
was one of the least offensive things, frankly. The men
who come in the middle of the night try worse things.

Jax wants to take me out for a drink. Yes, yes, yes,
I say to myself. Say yes. You deserve this. But I reject
him. I want to say yes, more than anything, but I
can't. I'm too fragile to have my heart broken by the
likes of him. Of course it would happen. He's cocky
and rich and arrogant, and guys like that only want
one thing. The thing that I certainly want to have
with him, but not now. Not considering everything
else I have that's going on.

The following day, just as the sun throws its
harshest rays on our dusty part of the world, my
mind drifts back to Jax. If only he would walk back
into this place. If only he would ask me again. Then
maybe I would say yes. But it's all a daydream.

My mind drifts from one part of his body to
another. He's got the kind of veins lining his
forearms that make me wet in my panties. I want to
pull off that two hundred dollar T-shirt and run my
fingers over his chiseled abs. I want to grab both of

his butt cheeks at the same time and get down on my knees before him.

"Sophia?"

A familiar voice startles me and brings me back down to earth. It's Jax. He's casually leaning on the countertop and tapping his fingers.

"Hey," he says.

"Hey."

I'm at a loss for words. My mouth gets parched.

"So I was in the neighborhood, and I thought I'd stop by."

"Oh, okay." I smile. "Can I get you a menu?"

"You can, but I'll just get whatever you recommend anyway."

His cockiness is oozing out of him. I look around. His friends are nowhere to be found, but the Bentley is parked in the first available non-handicapped parking spot.

"Where are your friends?" I ask.

"Not here." He smiles.

"Why are you?"

He takes a breath. "Like I said, I was passing through the neighborhood."

I roll my eyes.

"You don't believe me?"

"No." I shake my head. This guy is dangerous. In a good way. No, in a bad way.

"Well, take a seat. Anywhere you want," I say.

He looks around the café. There are three other people here. The lunch 'rush' just left, meaning the four other people who typically pop in for lunch. Jax chooses the seat at the counter. Right in front of me.

I grab a rag to pick up the few crumbs left over by the last customer and notice that my book is still in my hand.

"Jane Eyre." He nods. I hide the book behind the counter and wipe the counter around him. He doesn't move his arms and I stop to see if he will. He takes a moment before lifting his arms.

"You were reading that yesterday," he says. I nod and get my pad out. I can't find my pen and frantically look for it at the cash register. I can feel his gaze burning a hole in the back of my jeans. He's checking out my ass. I don't want to admit it, but I like it. A lot.

"Yes, I'm not done yet. Have you read it?"

"Yes, in school. It has a good story. Love and tension. Lots of awkward situations. It just needs something."

"You think a classic of English literature needs something? Seriously?" My tongue often gets away from me, but this is one of those situations where I don't really care. I love talking about literature, and he was the one who brought it up.

"Yes, so what?" He shrugs.

I shake my head at his arrogance. He's an asshole, and he knows it. He also knows that in some situations, like this one, it's ridiculously hot.

"So what does Jane Eyre need? How would you improve on Emily Brontë's masterpiece?"

"Hey, I'm not saying it's bad. I'm just saying that it's missing something that would really make it complete."

I cross my arms over my chest and wait for him to answer my question. This should be good.

"It needs sex. Lots of sex."

I stare at him.

"They have so much sexual tension. They are cooped up in this house together. They have all of these feelings developing for one another. We, as the audience, need a release. We need them to have sex. And lots of it."

I can hardly believe what I'm hearing.

"That's crazy." I shake my head. "Jane Eyre doesn't need sex."

"Oh, yes, she does. C'mon, aren't you just aching to read about them doing it?"

"Doing it? In Jane Eyre? Tempting, but no," I say definitively. How crude and vulgar and insulting can he be?

"Okay, it doesn't have to actually use those words. It can be much more poetic than that. But still as graphic."

"Like what, for example?"

He takes a moment to think about it. I wonder if he's going to choose a metaphor or go straight for a direct and honest description.

"How about this?" Jax leans back from the counter, tilting his head back. He lifts up his hand in the pose I've only seen professors do in movies.

"He slid himself into that heavenly place between her legs."

The words dangle in the air between us as if they are suspended by a string. I don't say anything for a moment. I'm speechless. I want to be embarrassed, but I'm more turned on than anything.

"So both graphic and romantic is your suggestion?" I finally say.

He nods. "I thought that struck an interesting tension between the two, depicting both his masculinity and her femininity in just the right way."

I smile and blush. I think so, too.

"You know you can't really talk like this in a public place," I say.

"Well, I'd love to go somewhere private." He leans closer to me.

His confidence is exuberant. I want to say yes. More than anything, I want to say yes. I want him to take me somewhere private and have his way with me.

"I'm sorry," I start.

"Aw, why?" He leans even closer and runs his fingers over my hand. I want to grab it and pull him close to me. I want to kiss his luscious lips and suck his tongue into my mouth.

But I pull my hand away.

"I just can't, not now."

"When? Why?" At that moment, Jax's deep set eyes resemble those I've seen in photographs of the Great Depression. Lost. Forgotten. Broken.

I can't explain. He's a stranger, and I feel like if I say *it* out loud to someone, I will burst out crying and never stop.

CHAPTER 13 - JAX

Her words pierce through my heart. Now I want her even more. I thought that things would be different since I came alone. I left my brothers back home and drove two hours back to this godforsaken town to see her again. She doesn't know this, of course. I hate the feelings of helplessness that she evokes in me. Why? Why didn't she say yes this time?

I have to have her. I crave her. I need to make her beg.

I look at Sophia. She stares at me with a blank stare that's impossible to read. She brings me my food and disappears back into the kitchen. She's not staying around to talk. I have no reason to eat at this shitty place without her presence.

"Don't take it personally," an older woman with a lifelong smoker's voice says.

She has been sitting at the far end of the counter all this time, but I didn't notice her until now. The woman comes closer. She smells of cigarettes and wears a small white apron with pockets, just like Sophia. There's no dress code here, but I know she's a waitress. Her name tag is old and worn, and I can't read her name.

"Sophia's going through a lot."

I nod as if I understand. The old woman is thin but looks as strong as an ox. She leans over the counter.

"Sophia just doesn't want more complications in her life right now," she whispers.

"What do you mean?"

"You know about her mom, right?"

"Yes," I lie.

"Well, she's getting worse. Neither of them can afford the chemo treatments anymore, and the insurance cap ran out a few months ago. It's looking really grim."

I nod. Her mom's dying of cancer.

"There's some experimental procedure that's available and looks like it could be an excellent option for her."

"That's good," I say.

"Yeah, except that Sophia can't afford it. She can't even come close."

"How much does it cost?"

"Not sure. Thousands. A couple hundred or so, I heard. And who's got that kind of money?"

I look away. My gaze drifts outside to my Bentley. That car costs as much as a cancer treatment to save someone's life. I've never put it in that perspective before.

The old woman startles me when she puts her long shriveled up fingers on my face and turns it toward her.

"So don't take it personally, kid. She's got a lot on her mind. But I know she likes you. I saw the way she was looking at you. In the seven years that I've known her, I've never seen her look like that at a guy before."

resent Day...

IT'S HIM. How could it be him? My mouth drops open and tears start to well up in my eyes. A big lump forms at the back of my throat. Why is it him?

"Are you okay?"

I shake my head no. And I don't think I'll ever be okay. No, no, no. It can't be him.

"How are you...Mr. Grayson?"

"Fine," he says slowly.

"No." I shake my head. "I mean...how is it that you are Mr. Grayson? I mean, I got the money from a foundation. I had no idea that it was...you."

"I know." He looks down at the floor. His hair falls slightly into his eyes. When he looks back at me, I feel as if he can see right through me. "That's the way I wanted it. I'm sorry. I mean, I'm sorry for not telling you sooner. I just wanted you to take the money."

I shake my head and wrap my hands around my shoulders.

"You thought that I wouldn't take it?" I ask after a moment. He looks deep into my eyes.

"Yes, I thought you would be too...proud."

I clench my jaw. I hate that he is right. I would've been too proud. Or maybe not. It is my mother who was sick, not me. I definitely wouldn't have taken it if it were just me.

"How is it that you know so much?" I ask. "About me?"

Now, it's his turn to be taken aback.

"I don't. Not really. I just saw you at that diner and...I wanted to know more about you."

"So you paid for my mom's cancer treatments? In what world does that make sense?"

He shrugs again.

"Why did you wait two years?"

"I wanted to know that your mother got better. For good."

"Why am I here now, Jax?" I ask.

"You remember my name."

Of course, I remember your name, I say to myself. I remember you from the diner. We don't always have attractive millionaires, or is it billionaires, just pop in for a bite to eat.

"Why am I here *now*, Jax?" I repeat my question.

"What do you mean?" he asks nonchalantly. As if he has nothing to explain. Nothing to hide.

"Why am I here?" I shrug. "What do you want from me?"

He shifts his weight from one foot to another and looks down.

"I don't know. I don't really have an answer," he finally says.

"You don't? You brought me all the way over here, and you don't have an answer?"

"No, not really." He shakes his head. "I just wanted you to come. You didn't want to go out with me..."

He doesn't finish his sentence. I wait for him to complete it.

"I didn't want to go out with you, so you decided to bring me here for a year. Force me to work for you?"

That gets his attention. And insults him, judging from how red his face gets.

"You are free to leave anytime, Ms. Cole." Jax looks straight at me. "You're not my slave. Who do you think I am?"

I shake my head. Now it's my turn to get incensed. "No, I can't. Not really, though," I say.

"Yes, you can."

"You paid for Mom's very expensive treatment, Jax. I really appreciate it. Why? Why did you do that?"

"Because I heard that she needed help. You needed help."

"But there are millions of people in the world to help. Why me?"

"Okay, there you got me." He shrugs. "I did it because I like you. I wanted to help you. I didn't want you to lose her. I heard she's doing really good."

"Yes, she is. And I'm very grateful for that. I want you to know that I am."

"Great, that's what I wanted to hear."

"But I still don't understand this." I wave my hands in between both of our chests. He grabs my hands and wraps his warm, strong fingers around each wrist. My heart skips a beat. I feel a surge of electricity pass through him to me. It's just a spark, but it makes me feel warm all over. All the shivers and uncertainty that I'd felt before dissipates. Now, I just want him to kiss me. I want him to keep holding my wrists and for him to slam his body into mine.

"What are you doing?" I whisper. I don't know how long he's been holding my wrists, but I never want him to stop.

"I wanted you..." he whispers. Jax takes a beat and looks straight into my eyes. "I want you."

That's it. The words just hang there in between us. I don't want to breathe in or out for fear that I will make them dissipate.

"You want me?" I whisper. He stares at me. "You want me to do what?" I ask.

"Nothing." He shrugs. "Nothing you don't want to do. I just want you here."

I nod. I don't understand, but I don't really need to right now.

There's a knock at the door.

"Mr. Grayson? Ms. Cole?" Mr. Whitewater says. "Dinner is ready."

———

"THANK you for wearing one of the dresses," Jax

whispers over my shoulder as I follow Mr.
Whitewater down the hallway. "I know it wasn't easy
for you."

I turn back. How does he know that? What the
hell do you know about me? I want to ask, but I
know he's right.

"I don't want to make you mad. I just want to say
thank you. You look stunning."

"You are welcome," I say. Though I have no idea
why he's thanking me for it.

"It's just such a treat for me," Jax explains as if he
knows what I was thinking.

His words send shivers up my spine.

The large twelve-person table that I had seen in
the dining room earlier that day is gone. We sit at
opposite sides. It's elegantly set with sparkling
silverware and crystal glasses. The plates are ivory
white, and the pottery is so magnificent, I can't help
but touch it.

"I love these plates," I say, running my fingers
over the middle of my plate. Then I realize that this
is probably really not polite. "I'm sorry, I shouldn't
have done that," I say, embarrassed.

"No, it's okay." Jax laughs. "I didn't know
someone could love plates."

I stare at him as if he were speaking a foreign

language. "What are you talking about? These are magnificent! Look at how many little man-made imperfections there are in the middle. These are not factory made. They are crafted by an artisan. A very gifted artist."

He smiles at me. "You know, you're quite a surprise, Sophia."

After placing the white napkin on my lap, I look at the bubbles rising to the top of the champagne glass. They dance in the candlelight, making my mouth water.

"This is delicious," I whisper, taking a sip.

"Yes, it's quite good." Jax smiles.

I reach for a large succulent strawberry from the middle of the table. Right before I grab it, Mr. Whitewater rushes over and helps me with it. My face gets flushed. I'm immediately embarrassed by my manners. But as soon as I pop it into my mouth, its exploding flavor overwhelms my senses.

"Oh. My. God," I whisper, shaking my head. I finish the strawberry in two massive and not very lady like bites.

"I'm glad you like them," Jax says. "We grow the strawberries ourselves. They're fresh from the garden."

CHAPTER 15 - JAX

WHEN I MAKE A MISTAKE…

*S*he sits across from me, staring at my mother's plates. She is doe-eyed, and I want nothing more than to grab her and kiss her. Her innocence is enchanting and contagious. She's making me look at the plates my mother has bragged about for ages in a completely new way.

"You know, these plates are from Mexico," I say. "My mother brought them back with her many years ago. Apparently, they are quite unique and expensive because they are so plain. Mexican pottery isn't known for that."

Sophia's eyes open even wider than before. Now I have her full attention. I just wish we weren't talking about fuckin' plates.

"Oh, wow," she says, running her fingers lightly

against the grain of her plate. I want more than anything to be that plate. I want her to run her fingers so carefully and lovingly along every inch of me.

"Jax?"

"Huh?" I come back to reality. Unfortunately.

"I just asked if you know what time period these are from."

"Oh, before the revolution. Mexican revolution. So, at least at the beginning of last century."

When can we stop talking about the goddamn plates?

Finally, Mr. Whitewater emerges with two servants, carrying two dishes.

"Pine nuts and kale salad with strawberries." Mr. Whitewater presents the food.

Sophia smiles and the world lights up.

"This looks delicious," she whispers and smiles at me, and then back at Mr. Whitewater.

I pick up my glass to make a toast, but she has already dug into her salad.

"Oh, I'm so sorry." She swallows quickly and drops her fork. Her crudeness makes me horny.

"No, it's okay. I just wanted to say thank you for joining me here. It's a pleasure."

I have a whole speech planned out, but I leave it

at that. She waits for me to continue, but I don't. Something is making me tongue-tied. I'm never tongue-tied.

"Thank you." She smiles. We clink glasses.

We don't speak much through the rest of dinner, and when we do we are consumed with formalities. By the time the dessert arrives, I realize that this wasn't the best idea. I shouldn't have made this dinner so formal. She feels awkward, and her awkwardness is making me feel uncomfortable. Politeness and formalities aren't her style. They're not mine either. But it had worked on so many girls before that I had convinced myself that it's the safe way to go.

"Are you okay?" Sophia asks as I walk her back to her room after dinner. She walks a few steps ahead of me, and I watch the way the taffeta under the dress bounces as she walks.

"Yes, of course." I smile. "Did you have a good time?"

"Yes, I did." Sophia smiles at me. "Dinner was delicious."

"And besides dinner?"

"You mean with you?"

I nod.

"Yes, I had a good time. To tell you the truth, I'm

really glad you didn't end up being some eighty-year-old creep."

I smile and nod. Her eyes twinkle in the dim hallway light. They are pulling me closer.

I take a step forward, and she takes a step back. Suddenly, there's nowhere to go. Her head hits the back of the wall. I take another step forward.

I take her chin and tilt her head toward mine. Our lips touch, and I run my tongue on the side of her lips. She tastes like honey and lavender. I pull her face closer to mine, and she wraps her hands around my shoulders. I get hard and bury my legs in her taffeta dress.

Our kisses grow stronger and more powerful. My fingers run down her back and up again toward her neck. Then they make their way to the front of her body. She tilts her head back, lost in passion. I run my lips down her neck as my hands cup her breasts and pull down on the straps of her dress.

"Jax," Sophia whispers.

"Sophia," I moan, kissing her neck. The urgency in my kisses intensifies, and I run my fingers up her naked leg.

"Jax," she says, pressing into me. I push back on her and continue to kiss her.

"Jax, stop," she says.

"No, no, no," I whisper, continuing to kiss her.

"Jax, stop!" she yells loud into my ear and knees me in the groin.

Shooting pain surges through my body, and I drop to the floor.

"What the hell, Jax?" Sophia yells, her eyebrows furrowed in anger.

"I'm sorry..." I whisper. I can't say it any louder. I'm lying on my back in the fetal position on the floor. I hear Sophia go into her room and lock the door. After a few moments, the pain subsides, and I manage to scramble up to my feet.

I knock on her door. No one answers. I knock again, and for some reason try the doorknob.

"It's locked, you asshole!" Sophia says.

"I'm sorry. I'm really, really sorry, Sophia."

"Go away!"

"Please, Sophia. I'm really sorry. You don't have to let me in..."

"I know that! I mean, what did you think? You invite me here, get me a pretty dress, wine and dine me, and I'll just do whatever you want? I'm not a whore, Jax."

"I know," I say. "I never meant for it to look like that. I just got carried away. I thought we were both feeling something, Sophia. I didn't mean to take it too far."

"Well, you did. And you're an asshole. When a girl says no, it means no. Keep that in mind for the future."

I'm so embarrassed. I can't believe this happened. I can't believe I did that.

"I honestly thought that we were both into it, Sophia. Please. You've got to believe me." My voice cracks a bit at the end.

"Fuck you!" Sophia says. "Oh, yeah, and I'm leaving tomorrow morning."

She can't. I will stop her. She has no right. "You are?" I ask. Please don't, I say silently.

"I've decided that I'm not in debt to you," she says. "You paid for my mom's treatment knowing that I could never pay you back. And I'm not going to sleep with you. Not even for a quarter of a million dollars. Not for any amount of money."

She's right, of course. I did all that knowing that. I just thought that maybe as a thank you. No, that's not right. I want her to want me. I don't want her to just sleep with me once. There's something about her that makes me want more. It's like she has some sort of spell on me.

"Okay," I finally say. "I understand. I'm leaving now."

I walk back to the library. I don't know where I'm headed. I'm just lost. Distraught. Ashamed. Who was that person back there? Not me, for sure. Sophia's right. I was an asshole. Am an asshole. She deserves much better than that. Who knows how far I would've taken it if she hadn't kneed me in the balls.

"Agh, I'm such an idiot." I say out loud. The words echo across the library chamber.

I hit my fist on the built-in bookshelves.

"Dammit!" I say. Now my hand is hurting, and my heart is pounding even faster than before. I take a deep breath and look up.

The bookshelves are stacked three high with old books, but only one stands out. Charlotte Brontë's *Jane Eyre*. The library is poorly lit, but this book seems to have a spotlight on it. I look out of the window and see the bright yellow moon looming high in the sky.

She'll like this, I decide. I pick up the first edition and flip through the pages. She won't be able to throw this gift away, I decide.

There's my grandfather's old writing desk in the corner. I sit down and open the top. I take a small piece of decorative paper from the top shelf and pick up the old ink pen, which miraculously still writes.

Sophia,

This is a first edition of Jane Eyre. *I hope you like it. I hope you accept this gift as my apology. I'm sorry.*

Love,

Jax

I READ THE NOTE OVER. Of course, she will know it's a first edition. It says so in the front. I ball up the piece of paper and toss it in the trash can.

Sophia,

I'm sorry. I didn't mean to do any of that this evening. Well, that's not true. I did mean to kiss you. I loved kissing you. I loved tasting you on my lips – I want to taste your sweet cunt.

I READ this note over again and again then crumple it up. This is supposed to be an apology. And like all apologies, it will have to be partly true and partly untrue. I can't say everything I want to say. Otherwise, she won't accept it.

I write another note. My final note. When I'm finished, I wait for the ink to dry before carefully folding it and placing it in front of the title page. In the back of the writing desk, I find a small box, which ends up being a perfect fit for the book. Now it really looks like a gift.

I walk back to Sophia's room and knock on the door. She doesn't answer. I don't know if she can hear me, but I decide to leave the box right outside. After trying one last time, I finally give up and walk away.

I've done all I could. At this point, I have no choice but to accept her decision. Whatever it might be. No matter how much I hate it.

CHAPTER 16 - SOPHIA

WHEN HE TRIES TO MAKE THINGS RIGHT…

I spend the night crying into my pillow. How dare he do that to me? I sob. My pillow is damp from all the tears I shed. I'm not just crying over what happened. I'm crying over what it means. He was such an asshole, and now I can never trust him again. I had to physically push him off me. Who the hell does that? How far would he have gone if I wasn't strong enough to push him away? To knee him in his balls?

Millions of thoughts swirl in my head. I hate him. And I want to kiss him. And I want to punch him. I want him to knock harder on my door and knock it down. And I want him to go away and leave me alone. My makeup is running down my face, and my eyes burn from all the cheap mascara getting into them. Finally, when they start to burn so much that it becomes unbearable, I force myself to go to the bathroom and wash my face.

"Why do you have to be such an asshole?" I say to myself in the mirror as if I'm talking to Jax. "We had such a great dinner. You were lovely. Polite. I was kind of a mess, but you weren't. You were...a gentleman. And then that. That happened. How can I forgive that?"

I shake my head. No, I can't forgive that because next time it might be much worse. I sigh.

I tried. I really tried. I came here. I had dinner. I even kissed him. This is all that he could've expected from me. It's okay if I go now. I've tried to repay my debt. It didn't work out. Because of *him*. So it's not my fault, right? Right.

There's a knock at the door. Then another. And another. I don't answer. I've said enough. I don't want to argue anymore. My mind is made up. In the morning, Mr. Whitewater is ordering me a cab or a driver, and I'm getting out of here.

———

THE FOLLOWING MORNING, I sleep in late. Late for me, anyway. I'm still in bed at eight a.m. The bed is made of feathers and softness beyond my imagination. I feel like I've slept on a cloud, and I'm not looking forward to going home to my thin, uncomfortable mattress at home. I got it for ninety-nine dollars on sale, and it feels like it.

I pull on the most comfortable pair of jeans I own and my favorite turquoise tank top. Someone once told me that I looked great in turquoise, and I've stocked my closet with turquoise tops ever since. I always thought they were right, but this morning, I'm not so sure. I look pale and tired. A big part of me is regretting the fact that I'm leaving, but I'm not sure I have the courage to go back on my word.

There's a light knock on the door.

"Who is it?"

"Good morning, Ms. Cole," Mr. Whitewater says after I open the door.

"Good morning, Mr. Whitewater," I say with a yawn.

He looks like he has been awake for hours. His hair is perfectly groomed and coiffed, and his suit is starched and ironed, or whatever one does to suits to keep them wrinkle-free.

"Mr. Grayson told me that you will be leaving this morning. I'm sorry to hear that."

"Yes, me, too." I nod. I am sorry. I wish this weren't happening.

He doesn't say another word, doesn't make a move either. I stare at him. What's wrong? Slowly, his eyes tilt down. I follow them to the floor and see a light pink box.

"Oh, what's this?" I ask.

"I'm not sure. But it's for you," Mr. Whitewater says. He quickly takes a step back and turns away from me to give me some privacy.

I examine the box carefully in my hand. The cardboard looks old and smells a bit like cake. I carefully open the flap and peek in. It's a book. A book?

I pull out the book and let the box drop to the floor. Oh my God. My heart starts to pound. Is this really what I think it is?

A first edition of *Jane Eyre*?

The book is rather small and weathered, but otherwise it's in excellent condition. I open it and run my hand along the smooth spine. I flip through the pages until I get some resistance at the very front. The pages are thicker here. Carefully, I flip the pages one at a time until I get to the title page and discover a note. It's written on perfumed paper, the kind that you see in expensive paper stores. There's a delicate floral design gracing each of the ends.

I open the note.

It's from Jax. I see his name written in beautiful, careful script on the bottom.

D EAR S OPHIA,

I'm sorry. For everything.

You deserve a lot better than me, of course. But please give me another chance.

Y OURS,

Jax

Y OURS. I like the sound of that. I've never had anyone who was mine in that way. My heart skips a beat again. And then another.

Mr. Whitewater clears his throat, and I remember that he's still here.

"I think I need a moment, Mr. Whitewater," I finally manage to utter. I go back into my room and close the door.

"Oh my God," I whisper. "A first edition of
Jane Eyre!"

I press the hardback book to my breasts and
inhale its beautiful musty smell. This book has been
around for hundreds of years, and now it's mine. It
belongs to me.

But can I accept it if I decide not to stay here? I
want to. He owes me an apology, and this is a
marvelous apology.

My thoughts drift back to Jax. Suddenly, I
remember the softness of his lips and how they
danced with mine to a tune that only we heard. I
remember how hot I felt in between my legs and
how much I wanted him to push up my taffeta skirt
and let me wrap my legs around his strong, powerful
torso.

He wasn't alone in feeling what he was feeling. I
was there, right along with him. We shared a
chemical and electric connection. I was drawn to
him as if he were a magnet, and I had trouble
pulling away as well. I loved feeling his hardness
pushing against me, pressing me to the wall. I
wanted to rip off his clothes. I wanted him to rip off
mine. And then it was just too much. In a split
second, it was suddenly too much.

CHAPTER 17 - SOPHIA

WHEN THERE'S AN ACCIDENT…

I don't know what I should do. I want to stay, but I also want to go. I want to stay to get to know Jax more. And I want to run away from this place and its games.

The sound of a startled horse scares me, and I walk over to the window. I lift the window and open the shutters. I didn't notice it last night, but there are stables to the right of me. The horse makes another piercing cry, sending shivers over my body.

"It's okay, Sebastian. It's okay, guy," Jax says. I can't see him, but his voice is firm and commanding, and I really believe that it's going to be okay.

Suddenly, they emerge. Jax is dressed in jeans, a pair of brown boots, and a simple white T-shirt. He's tan, and his sweaty body glistens in the sun. His hair looks wet, either from sweat or water. He's riding a tall black horse with a thick black mane that flies up with each gallop. They are moving as one. I look closer, and I see that the horse is not wearing a saddle. Jax is riding bareback.

The horse and the rider dance together for a few moments in a circle. The horse kicks up swirls of dust, which in the sunlight look like periwinkle. Then suddenly, the horse shifts his weight and raises his front legs in the air.

"Oh, wow," I whisper in awe. Jax remains in place on his back holding on by nothing but his powerful thighs. It looks like the horse is going to land on his front legs and morph into a trot, but he doesn't. Instead, he lands hard on his front hooves and lifts his back hooves up high in the air. Then he does it all again.

My smile fades quickly after I realize that something's going wrong.

"Oh my God," I whisper and bring my hands to my face. "No, no, no..."

But it's too late. The horse bucks one last time, and this time Jax doesn't hold on. I see him flying through the air. He misses the chain-link fence by less than a foot and lands flat on his back.

"Oh my God!" I scream. My voice echoes around the room, but Jax doesn't get up.

"Get up! Please get up!" I scream, but he doesn't.

For a brief second, I consider running to the back of the room, down the long hallway, down the winding staircase, out of the front door, and around the entire ten thousand square foot house, but then I see a simpler way down.

"What are you doing?" Mr. Whitewater enters my room.

I'm already hanging out of the window, half of my body is on the roof of the patio.

"Jax is hurt, call 911!"

I climb down the post of the patio, jump into the orange grove below and run toward Jax.

I finally reach him. His face is so pale that it's the color of those white Mexican plates from dinner. All the blood has drained from his face, and his lips are blue.

"Jax? Jax?" I scream. I want to shake him and bring him back to life. But I'm afraid he has broken something in his body, and that will make it worse.

"Jax? Jax? Please wake up. Please, please, please!" I shout, cradling my arms around him.

Mr. Whitewater runs over.

"How is he? Oh my God. He's unconscious."

I nod. I don't know what else to do.

"I just called 911, but they won't be here for some time."

"What, why?" I demand to know.

"Twenty minutes at the earliest," he says and puts the receiver back to his ear. "They say that we shouldn't move him until they get here. He might've broken his back."

The world fades to black with those words. 'He might've broken his back' is all I hear in my head over and over again. The paramedics arrive sometime later. They have to scream at me to get out of the way. I don't move. I don't even know if I can move. Someone pushes me out of the way, and they take Jax away. They strap him onto a gurney and roll him to the ambulance.

I can't go along. No one can. They tell me and Mr. Whitewater that we can follow along behind the ambulance if we want.

I'm in a daze. I don't know what to do. I follow Mr. Whitewater to his car.

"Are you sure you want to come? I thought you were leaving?"

I stare at him. All thoughts of leaving have all but dissipated. I don't even know what he's talking about. All I know is that I can't leave now. I don't know what's wrong with him, and I can't leave until I find out. What if he needs my help?

———

I'VE SPENT the last twelve hours in the hospital looking at magazines and mindlessly reading books that I did not understand on my phone. I read the words, but they don't make any sense. I don't know who wrote them or for what reason. The only thing that makes sense to me is the pictures. I leaf through the celebrity magazines and pay close attention to which movie stars have lost and gained weight. Which ones are pregnant. Which ones got engaged and which ones got divorced. It's all things that I used to find interesting, but now none of it makes any sense.

This hospital reminds me of the one back home where I waited for hours for my mom to get out of her various surgeries. Time stands still here. It's as if the waiting room is some secret time travel chamber in which I can go into and not age for hours and days and months. I age, of course. I noticed it whenever I went into the bathroom and looked at the horror that was my face, but I never felt time passing. Not even one second.

Breathe, I say to myself. Breathe.

I take a deep breath. And then another. And another. I feel a little better, but as soon as I look around, all of my thoughts and concerns and regrets creep back in.

A doctor who is in charge of Jax and his condition comes out from behind the double doors with a smile on his face.

"Jax is awake now," he tells Mr. Whitewater. "He's one lucky young man. Even though both of his legs are broken."

Broken legs. I sigh. He is lucky.

"Wait here," Mr. Whitewater tells me. I have no right to go see Jax. I'm not really anybody to him. Barely an employee. Still, I hope that I can go in to see him.

"And he doesn't have any brain damage?" Mr. Whitewater asks the doctor.

"No, not that I can tell. But it's too soon to know for sure."

I wait for what seems like a century for Mr. Whitewater to come back. Now time is positively moving backward. I wonder if it's 1993. Finally, he comes out.

"He'd like to see you," Mr. Whitewater says.

"How is he?"

"Fine. Definitely all there."

I smile. A wave of relief sweeps over me.

CHAPTER 18 - JAX

Sophia walks into my hospital room carefully and cautiously. It's as if she's walking on eggshells.

"It's okay," I say. "Don't be afraid." I sit up in my bed, trying not to look so sickly and powerless, even though I have a pounding headache.

"How are you?" she asks sheepishly.

Her hair falls into her face slightly as she walks, and she pushes it aside without much regard. Her lips look soft and exquisite even under the harsh fluorescent lights of the hospital room. Her skin is tan, and her cheeks are full of color. Sophia is wearing a long sleeve hoodie, and she wraps her arms around her shoulders as if she is trying to hold on to the entire world.

"I'm good. Fine," I say confidently. It's almost true. I want it to be true. I'll act like it is until it becomes true.

"Broke both legs," I say, nudging at the casts. "Imagine the luck."

"It could've been much worse, Jax." She comes closer. I love the sound of my name in her mouth.

"Nah." I wave my hand. But she slaps it away.

"No, I'm serious. It could've been much, much worse. I saw you out there. You passed out. You were unconscious. I thought you would go into a coma and never wake up."

"Hah, like you'd care. You'd just be happy that you got off the hook," I joke.

She stares at me and raises her hand to slap me again. This time across the face. But something stops her.

"Fuck you, Jax. Fuck you for even thinking something that terrible."

That was a pretty shitty thing to say. I shake my head. "I'm sorry. I didn't mean that. I was just trying to make you laugh."

"How would that make me laugh, exactly?"

"I don't know. I'd shrug, but my shoulders hurt too much."

This one does make her laugh. She opens her

lips just a bit and lets out a small, willowy laugh. The world is alright again.

————

"How did this happen?" Sophia asks after a few silent moments.

"That's what you get for riding a young stallion bareback." I laugh.

Her face turns white. "What do you mean? Are you joking again?"

I shake my head no. Then suddenly, something comes over me, and I tell her something I never would otherwise.

"I was really upset that you were leaving. That I did that to you. Disrespected you like that. But I want you to know that it was really an accident. I must've not heard you or something. I would never keep going beyond what you said was okay. I'm not that guy."

I stop and look at her. She waits for me to continue.

"So I was really angry with myself over the whole thing. Over what I did. Over the fact that you were now scared of me. And leaving. That's the last thing I wanted. So this morning, I went for a walk and

ended up in the stables. I saw Sebastian. He's a
powerful thoroughbred. But he's not broken yet. He's
wild and crazy, and I felt wild and crazy at that
moment. It was like we were breathing the same air
and feeling the same energy. I opened the gate, and
he let me get on top of him. I really thought we were
connecting, and we wanted the same thing. But I
was just feeling crazy. He ignited something within
me, some long forgotten feeling of hope and love
and wildness. And so I urged him outside of the
stable. And that's when it got bad. He started to
buck, and he wouldn't slow down long enough for
me to get off. And then I just flew off."

"You remember it all?"

"I remember every single moment."

"And what about afterward?"

"No." I shake my head. "Once I hit the ground, I
don't remember anything."

She looks at me. Tears well up inside of her eyes.
One large tear breaks free and rolls down her cheek.
I reach out and wipe it off her face.

"I was so scared, Jax. You were just lying there.
Motionless. Unconscious. I wanted to shake you so
much, but I was afraid something was broken.
And then..."

Her voice drops off, and she looks out of the

window. A tiny sparrow dances on a branch. We both watch the sparrow for a moment before she turns back to me.

"And then?" I ask.

"And then I thought that maybe it was even worse than that. You didn't wake up, Jax. Not for a long time."

I nod.

"You scare me, Sophia," I finally say.

"What do you mean?"

"I don't know exactly. But I feel something for you, and it scares me."

"Don't be silly." She waves her hand and smiles. "How can I scare you?"

I try to shrug again. Again I feel pain.

"Come here," I say and wave my index finger to get her to come closer to me.

"What?" She leans down.

"You scare me," I whisper and press my lips up to hers. I lift my body a bit toward hers and my neck throbs in pain.

I sigh in pain when I pull away.

"Are you okay?" she asks with a smile, licking her lips.

"No." I shake my head. "But it was worth it."

———

WHEN I WAKE up in the morning, my back is throbbing, and I find Sophia half asleep in the chair.

"Hey, you're awake." She smiles at me.

"What are you doing here?" I ask. "I can't believe you slept the whole night here."

"Oh, I just dozed off. It's no big deal."

"No, it is," I say. "Thank you."

"I'm going to get us some coffee." She jumps up to her feet.

I'm jealous of the spring in her step, and I wish more than anything that I could jump as well. I've only been in bed for one day, and the thought of not being active for another two months scares me to death.

"Sophia..."

She turns at the door. Her hair leaps one last time before landing softly around her shoulders.

"Yes?"

"I was just wondering..." I don't know how to phrase the question exactly. She waits for me as I try.

"I was just wondering if you were planning on going back home today?"

"No." She shakes her head. A wave of relief

sweeps over me, but I'm not sure if I have been clear enough.

"And tomorrow?" I ask.

Suddenly, it hits her what I'm asking. She walks back to my bed.

"I'm not going home for a while, Jax. But under one condition."

"What's that?"

"If you promise me that we will be friends. Just friends."

I think about that for a moment. Just friends is better than nothing. "Okay." I nod.

*H*ow do you know if you truly love someone?

There was a time in my life when I never believed in love. I grew up in a world of privilege. My brothers and my sister, Opal, were raised by our nannies and had everything we ever wanted. Our parents had houses in Los Angeles, New York, Montana, an apartment in Paris, and another one is being built in Dubai.

When we were little, the family had more cars than I could even count – our father, Dr. Grayson – is an avid collector. We each got a new car of our choosing as soon as we turned sixteen, and each one of us promptly crashed it soon after. I think it was my sister O who kept her first car, a brand new

Mercedes, the most expensive class of that year, the longest. Six months, I believe.

My mother never cooked, but every night that we had dinner at home, we always had a delicious gourmet meal prepared by our personal chef. Our birthdays were lavish and expensive. Each one probably cost as much as a regular couple's wedding. They were extravagant with different themes and costumes and close to four hundred guests each time. That doesn't sound like a fun birthday party for a five-year-old, but the entire school was invited so most of them were.

Our exclusive private school didn't have a school bus to get us to school, and the responsibility fell to our nannies to deliver us there and pick us up after each of our after-school activities. O did theater. My brothers and I played lacrosse.

Our parents were always there to cheer for us – always physically present – and yet emotionally and metaphysically away. It's hard to explain now, difficult to put into words, but it was as if they were never really there.

Ever since I can remember, our parents had their own lives. My father, the renowned doctor and later the founder and CEO of a prosperous pharmaceutical company, worked late into the night and all weekends. He was always traveling and running meetings.

My mother had her philanthropic activities. She was the head of a number of boards that raised money for a variety of noble causes. She didn't get paid, but she worked nearly as hard as he did and organized all of our days and the house staff on top of all that.

It's maybe cruel to say this, but my parents gave me the impression that love only meant one thing. My parents said that they loved us, but their love was complicated. It came with expectations and, inevitably, disappointments. It was never the kind of love often featured in movies. They were never mushy and hopeful and exuberant. They were both too busy with either work or their social obligations to really show love. Or at least, the way I expected it to be.

And so, coming back to my original thought. How do you know if you truly love someone? How am I expected to know if I love someone if their love was the only kind of love I had ever known?

Before I broke both of my legs riding a wild stallion, I never had time to think about these things. But now that I'm bed bound for more than six weeks, it seems all I do is think. I have to remain active somehow, and my mind is the only place I have left.

Sophia enters the room carrying two cups of tea on a tray. She has been here for six weeks. Six of the happiest weeks of my life. I have never been immobile for this long before, and yet her presence has made it, somehow, bearable. If it weren't for her, I'd be tearing my hair out. I'd be drunk all day just to pass the time. And yet, with her here, we find things to do that do not involve going outside much or using our legs.

———

I THINK I'm falling in love with Sophia. Her long hair, her tender eyes, her soft skin. I don't know anything about love, I'm the first to admit it. Yet, I also know that I've never felt this way about anyone before. Sometimes, when I see her, my heart jumps into my throat, and I forget to breathe.

Other times, when she's away from me for a couple of hours, I feel anxious and uncertain. I don't know what to do with myself and spend the hours just looking out of the window or staring aimlessly at the television screen. I can't read a word that makes sense. All I can do is wait for her to return.

Sophia has been bringing me breakfast, lunch, and dinner and has made Mr. Whitewater all but useless. The responsibility of those things would've fallen to him, but she asked him if she could do it. I think she likes being useful. In fact, I've never met someone who enjoys being useful so much. It's almost as if she really loves taking care of me.

I feel myself falling in love with Sophia, even though I'm not sure if I know what that means. But does anyone? Isn't love just some sort of feeling that bubbles up from within us, from someplace deep within our core that we didn't even know existed?

There is one problem, however. And it's a big one. We – Sophia and I – have decided to keep things professional. I believe that the only reason she's even here is that our relationship is now strictly professional. Or so she has called it. But in reality, it's not professional at all. Only a fool would think that our interaction is professional. We are more like friends. Close, close friends. And it's clear, at least I think it is, that I want more.

"What a beautiful morning, right?" she says, plopping down on the couch next to me. "What do you want to do today?"

I want to kiss you, undress, and lie in bed looking

at and exploring your naked body until dinner. I
want to say this to her, but instead I lie.

"Not sure, whatever." I shrug and remember her
hurtful words.

"No more kissing, no more romance, or whatever
it was that was happening between us," she said in
my hospital room. I felt woozy from all the pain
killers, but I remember each one of her words as if
she'd said it a minute ago. "I just want to work here
for the year, like I agreed, and be friends."

"Okay," I had agreed.

"You promise?" she asked. "This is one of my
conditions of staying. The only one."

I remember looking into her deep brown eyes
and nodding. Then agreeing verbally to the only
thing that would keep her in my life.

CHAPTER 20 - JAX

WHEN THINGS GET BETTER…

"*Y*ou feeling alright?" she asks. Neither of us has said a word in a few moments. She touches my hand with hers, sending shivers up and down my body. Ever since we'd decided to be friends, she's started touching me more and more. More than she ever had before. But the touching is not sexual, at least not on her part. Just a pat of the hand, a small hug, a nudge, but each touch still makes me get hard.

I want her. I want her up against the wall. On the bed. Outside in the desert. In the shower.

"Hey, Jax?" she asks, leaning close to me with a look of concern on her face. "How are you today? Is everything okay?"

"I'm good." I fake a smile. "Why?"

"Something seems off." She shrugs. "Oh, I almost forgot, I got your pills, here."

I stare at her. Sophia mentions the pills in the same nonchalant way she has for the last six weeks, but this is the first day that I turn them down.

"Nah, I'm feeling okay. I don't think I need them today."

Her face lights up. "That's great!" She wraps her arms around me. "I'm so happy. You're making so much progress. Maybe you'll be able to take the casts off soon, too."

Now there's a thought. To stand up and hold my body weight with my own two feet. I've taken that for granted for so many years. Then when I suddenly couldn't stand up on my feet and had to use crutches...the helplessness that came with that was unimaginable.

I smile with my whole body at the thought of taking the casts off.

"Yeah, I can't wait," I say. "I hate being a blimp. I feel like I'm totally useless. And like I'm getting fat."

Sophia laughs. It's a small, quiet laugh that only gives me a small peek at her perfect white teeth. Then she looks me up and down.

"No, not at all."

"You have no idea how hard this has been for me.

I mean, I know it hasn't been easy for you at all, waiting on me all the time. Which again, you don't really have to do. We have staff here for that," I say.

She starts to say something, but I cut her off. I know what she's going to say. She is the staff, she's happy to do it, or something in that vein.

"That's not what I want to say. What I mean is that it's been really hard for me to be so inactive for so long. I love being outdoors. I love riding horses. Playing basketball. Football. Baseball. Whatever. Using my body is a huge part of my life, and these past six weeks, it's like I've become someone else. I couldn't do that. And if it weren't for you…I would've been completely lost. It would've been much harder. So what I'm really trying to say, very artfully, is thank you. Thank you so much for being here. And being you."

Sophia takes a moment to internalize what I've said. Then she leans close to me. It takes all of my strength not to place my lips on hers, but I've long made myself a promise that it would be her, this time, who has to make the first move.

"It has been my pleasure," she whispers in my ear and pulls away.

———

SOPHIA JUMPS off the couch and the mood in the room changes. I watch her walk over to the large floor-to-ceiling window looking out onto the desert in front of us. A large raven perches on top of a crooked Joshua tree in the distance and then flies away.

"I finally found some tape, and I'm going to take care of that bird problem," she says. By bird problem, she means that too many birds are flying into our spotless window and killing themselves. Mr. Whitewater, who washes that window almost every other day, isn't going to be happy, and we both know it.

"You know he has been hiding this thing from me for all of these weeks," she says with a smile and picks up the roll of duct tape from the tray. "I've been asking him for it forever."

"What can I say, he loves keeping that window clean."

"I know he does, and the view from it is beautiful. But we can't just sit by and do nothing as birds continue to kill themselves on it practically every day."

"I guess not." I chuckle.

"Where do you think I should put it?" Sophia asks.

Over my hands and then to the headboard, so that I can't touch you as you go down on me. And then I will wrap it around your hands and do the same to you.

Of course, I don't say any of that out loud. Instead, I point to a few spots on the window, which have resulted in the largest amount of casualties.

"You know, I talked to my mother again this morning," Sophia says as she tapes the window.

"Oh, yeah, how is she?" I ask. I only mildly care. Don't get me wrong, I'm glad she's doing better but mainly because that means that Sophia doesn't have to go back home and take care of her.

"She's doing even better than before." She smiles.

The $250,000 check that I sent her for her mother's treatment was worth that smile alone. Sophia tells me more about her mom. Her breathing is improving. She doesn't have much pain in her hips, blah, blah, blah. All the information goes in one ear and out the other. I'm not paying attention. Not even a little bit.

Instead, my mind drifts elsewhere. I look at Sophia's round butt and the way it fills out her jeans. Her jeans have little decorative hearts on the back pockets, and they draw my eye to the roundest part of her body. I don't know why clothing designers put them there. Do they know that they make women's butts look irresistible? Is that the whole point? Do the women know just how hard it is to look away from those two little hearts? Does Sophia?

When she turns to face me and tell me something else about her mom's condition, my gaze runs up her body. Sophia's small waist accentuates her hips, making them appear wider than they really are. Then I land on her breasts. She doesn't wear a bra often, but her breasts are firm and erect. When the temperature in the room falls below seventy-five degrees Fahrenheit, her nipples get erect and resemble the tips of a ripe strawberry. I've gotten into the habit of turning down the furnace and praying each morning that today would be the day that she again chooses to go without a bra.

"Hey, are you listening?" Sophia asks.

"Yeah, so your mom is happy with the new doctor?" I parrot the last thing that she said to me. I developed this talent of reiterating the last line that someone said back in sixth grade, and it has served me well way after I was done with formal education.

My words put her at ease, and she continues on with her story while I curse myself for ever agreeing to be this hot girl's friend.

Fuck being friends!

We shouldn't be just friends.

Friends with benefits maybe.

Fuck buddies.

Lovers.

Girlfriend?

Fiancée even.

Maybe more.

I shudder at the places my mind is going. Girlfriend, maybe. I've had a few girls who I liked enough to call my girlfriend. But fiancée? Really, Jax? What are you thinking? That's exactly it, though. I'm not thinking. I'm just feeling.

CHAPTER 21 - SOPHIA

WHEN I NO LONGER WANT TO BE FRIENDS…

I don't know why the fuck I ever insisted on being friends with Jax. The friends status was supposed to protect me. It was supposed to make me feel safe and to make me feel as if nothing is going to happen between us. I thought that it would create distance between us and release some of the tension that forms whenever we occupy the same room. But it's only making things worse.

I want him.

I want him to want me.

He does. I can feel it. But he won't make a move. He made me a promise, and he's keen on keeping it.

Even now, standing on this stupid chair, taping tape onto the glass to stop the damn birds from crashing into it every day, I feel Jax's eyes burning a hole in my back pocket.

He's staring at my ass, and the scary thing is that I want him to, but more than that, I want him to grab it and pull me up to his lap and kiss me.

Of course, he won't. He has made a promise.

So now it's all up to me. And I'm afraid. And I'm a coward.

———

AFTER TAPING ALL the spots where birds have crashed into the past week, I get down and sit next to him on the couch, which has become his home. Jax hasn't moved much in weeks. He pretends that he's fine, but I can feel his anxiety growing.

"I need to get the hell out of here. Out of this room. Away from this couch. I want to see Sebastian again."

I get goose bumps at the thought. Sebastian is the crazy, untamed, three-year-old stallion that broke both of his legs the last time he tried to ride him. I don't want Jax anywhere near him. He was lucky to get out of that situation with only both legs broken. The doctors said it could've been much worse. He could've broken his back and ended up like Christopher Reeve.

"Can I ask you something?" I ask.

Jax nods and waits for the question.

"Why did you ever get on him in the first place? What were you trying to prove?"

I don't know much about horses, but I do know that no one in their right mind rides stallions. All the testosterone makes them crazy and wild. Unbroken.

"Nothing." He shrugs in the casual way that makes me swoon. "I just felt like riding him, that's all."

I don't believe him. "I don't think so," I say, staring straight into Jax's deep eyes.

"You don't? Why?"

"I think you were angry with yourself. And you wanted to, I don't know, take some of that anger out on yourself."

Jax's eyes meet mine. I can tell by the way he sits back in the couch and adjusts his stature that I've hit on something.

"Oh, please." He shrugs and rolls his eyes. He's lying. Either to just me or to the both of us.

"No, I do." I smile. "Really."

Then his face grows serious. The casualness that just danced across it all but disappears.

"Listen, Sophia," Jax says. All I hear is the irritation in his voice. "Please don't psychoanalyze me, okay? I've been through that enough with a ton of real doctors. The last thing I need is some more psychobabble from some novice."

His words sting. More than that even. They pierce my heart. I feel tears bubbling up and I'm about to let them all out.

"Fuck you," I say and leave before I show even more vulnerability.

"Sophia, I'm sorry. I'm sorry!" I hear Jax yell after me, but I don't turn around. At this moment, I hate him. I hate him the way I never hated anyone.

We don't speak the rest of the day. By the next day, my anger with Jax dissipates a bit. He apologizes again, and this time, I accept his apology. By the afternoon, we joke and laugh like before. I'm glad that things between us have improved, but I am still keenly aware of the boundaries that separate us. Now I'm also more cautious. Certain things can't be talked about or joked about.

That afternoon, over a very late lunch or an early dinner, I ask Jax about his family. He tells me about his domineering father and the pharmaceutical company that he started when all the kids were little.

"My father's got us kids, but that company was his real baby," he says. "And we all knew that for many years."

"What about your mom?" I ask.

"Mom was there and not there. She had her own commitments, but most of the time she was absent. It's like she had her own interests that none of us kids ever fit into."

"Not even Opal?" I ask. I know that mothers can often be closer to their daughters than to their sons.

"Not even O. We've all had nannies, though, so that was supposed to make up for everything, I guess. It felt like they loved me, all of us, I mean, in their own way, but it was somehow never enough. You know?"

I nod. I try to understand, but Jax and I come from two completely different worlds.

"What about you?" he asks. "What was it like for you growing up?"

I take a moment to consider the question.

"It wasn't really easy," I say. "My father left when I was little, when my little sister was only two."

"I didn't know you had siblings."

"I don't. Well, not anymore. I never know how to answer that question about brothers or sisters."

"What do you mean?" he asks. He moves closer to me with a steadfast look of concern on his face.

"Well, I used to have a sister until I was fifteen, but then she died. She was sick almost her whole little life and, after she passed, my mother was never the same after that."

"What did she die of?" he asks even though I have the feeling that he already knows.

"Cancer. What else?" I shrug.

"Like your mother?" he gasps.

I nod. "My mom was diagnosed soon after. Right when I graduated from high school. That's why I never went to college. She was the sole breadwinner and, after her diagnosis, she couldn't really work. Not with all the chemo and radiation. So I got a job at the diner. And then another one at a bar. And I've been sort of stuck there ever since."

I look at him. I like the way he looks at me. There's pity and sorrow on his face, but it isn't as depressing as the looks other people typically have.

"But it's okay now." I smile. "Thanks largely to you."

"I just wish that I'd met you earlier," he says.

A big part of me wishes that too. I've spent so

many years being poor and living paycheck to paycheck, on even less than a paycheck, that having money seemed like an answer to all of my problems. People like to say that money is not the answer to all of your problems, but for many years it would've been the answer to all of mine.

CHAPTER 22 - SOPHIA

WHEN I TELL HIM MY DREAMS…

We share more this day than any other day. I feel us growing closer and closer. Even if we don't fully comprehend or understand or conceptualize each other's childhood experiences, we are at least aware of them.

After we finish our salads, Mr. Whitewater brings us soup. I hand Jax his bowl and take mine. It's not very comfortable to eat soup on the couch, but I don't want to move.

"What did you want to be when you grew up?" Jax asks.

"I don't know," I say. "You mean for work? I thought I'd be lucky if I became a nurse or something like that. It would give me a steady job or profession. The pay is much better than a waitress's."

"No." He shakes his head. "That's not what I mean. Not just for work. Didn't you have dreams of what you wanted to do or to be when you were older? No matter how unrealistic."

I smile. I'm about to tell him that only wealthy or privileged kids spend their days thinking about unrealistic dreams and go about pursuing those, but then I really think about it and realize that I, too, had a dream once. And, perhaps, still do.

"Okay, I'll tell you, but only if you promise to keep it a secret."

"Keep it a secret? Don't you know that dreams can't become a reality unless you verbalize it? Unless you infuse them with the power of speech?"

"Actually, no, I didn't know that. But if you want to hear this then you have to promise."

He takes a moment, then agrees.

"I've never told anyone this before, but I want to be a doctor," I say.

"That's great! That's an amazing thing to want to be." Jax smiles with his whole face.

I feel overwhelmed by his exuberance.

"But why don't you want anyone to know? It's so inspiring and beautiful."

Inspiring and beautiful? I'm not so sure.

"Because it's embarrassing," I mumble.

"What? How?"

I stare at him. "I just don't think you understand because you were probably raised to think that you can be anyone you want. Do anything you want. Right? But I wasn't. I don't even have a bachelor's degree, Jax. Only a high school diploma."

"That's crap! Don't say that. Degrees don't matter. All that matters is whether or not you want to do it. And then you gotta take steps to do it."

"That's your privileged upbringing talking," I joke.

"No, it's not." He leans closer to me. His face gets really serious. "To be a doctor you need heart. And you have that. I think you can be a doctor if you really go after that. No, I *know* you can."

His words wash over me like a wave. Overwhelmed by his support and encouragement, I have trouble taking a full breath. A knot forms in the back of my throat. If I don't inhale slowly, I'm afraid that I won't be able to take a full breath again.

No one has ever believed in me so much before.

We both return to our food. Jax takes two last scoops of the soup. I lean across him to put the bowl on his side of the side table.

I've done this hundreds of times over the last six weeks, but today is different. There's a warmth emanating from Jax, the kind that I haven't felt since our last kiss. I watch him take a breath and inhale the world around us, the way people smell a bouquet of flowers.

When he opens his eyes, he catches me staring at him and sits back. He's giving me room to collect myself. He's respecting my boundaries and the rules that we have both agreed to play by. But this time, I don't – can't – respect those boundaries anymore. This time, I don't pull away. I look at his sweet, beautiful lips and press mine to them.

Immediately, his lips respond to mine. He pulls me closer to him and wraps his arms around my shoulders. In a split second, the whole world fades away. His hands move through my hair and my fingers run along his jawline. It's strong and powerful and touching it makes me want him even more.

"This is wrong," I whisper without pulling away.

"Yes, and yet it's so right," he mumbles.

And then suddenly, he stops and looks at me.

"Do you want to stop?" he asks. "Is that what you meant?"

Yes and no. I don't know.

He waits for me to answer, but I've lost the ability

to speak. Instead, I reach up to him again and run my tongue on the inside of his mouth.

"Oh, Sophia," he moans. He lifts up my head with his hands, then runs his hands down to my hips. With one swift motion, he lifts me up and places me on top of him.

I laugh and continue kissing him. I feel how hard he is, and it makes me feel tingly all over my body. He pulls away from my lips and starts to kiss down my neck. I tilt my head back and sigh from pleasure. His lips make their way down my collarbone and toward my breasts. He takes one of my breasts in his hand and kisses the top.

I close my eyes. I want this moment to last forever.

"Oh my, I'm so sorry!" A female voice shatters our bliss. I pull away from Jax but remain firmly on top of him.

"What the fuck are you doing here, O?" Jax yells out. His deep voice startles me, and I fall to the side. I scramble to adjust my clothes. When everything seems in place, I look back up.

There's a tall, gorgeous woman in five-inch heels standing before me. Her hair is jet black and cut in an aggressive slant. Her makeup is flawless, and her eyelashes are long and powerful. She has pale skin, and her blood red lipstick makes her look like something of a clash between a 50's pinup and a vampire.

"I live here, too, remember?" She laughs and tosses her hair. "Besides, I've come to see how you are feeling. And from what I can see, you're doing quite well."

Neither Jax nor I say a word. I probably look as dumbfounded as he does.

"Well, since my brother seems to have forgotten his manners, I'll introduce myself. I'm Opal, Jax's older sister."

Opal extends her hand to me. When I shake it, what strikes me most about it is how cold it is. Her fingers are long, and her long gray nails are filed down to a point at the end. In fact, come to think of it, everything about Opal is pointy. She has pointy heels, a pointy nose, pointy nails, and even pointy elbows.

"I'm Sophia. I'm Jax's personal assistant," I mumble.

"Yes, I see. You're definitely assisting him on a very personal level," she says, lifting one of her eyebrows.

"O, please. Play nice," Jax says. "Sophia's a friend."

Opal puts her sunglasses back over her eyes, turns on her heel, and waves her hand. "Well, I gotta get my bag."

Jax and I watch her walk out. Before she reaches the end of the hallway, she turns around briefly and says, "Sophia, can you help me with something here?"

I look at Jax, unsure as to what to do.

"No, O, take care of it yourself!" he yells back.

"No, it's okay." I get up. "I'll help her; it's no problem."

CHAPTER 23 - SOPHIA

$\mathcal{M}$r. Whitewater takes O's Louis Vuitton bags to a guest room upstairs and places them near the bed.

"You don't mind unpacking these for me, do you? Sophia, is it?" Opal asks, walking toward the door.

"What?" I ask. I'm not sure if I had heard that right.

"You work here, right? Or do you just get paid to fuck my brother?"

I stare at her.

"Hello? Earth to Sophia! Do you work here or not?"

"Yes," I mumble.

"Well, please unpack my bags for me then," she says and walks out.

I'm dumbfounded. I've never been treated like that by anyone. I'm not sure what to do. I look at her three bags. How dare she speak to me that way? I'm not a maid. I'm not a servant.

I want to toss her bags over the railing and punch her in her stupid face.

I sit down on the bed.

Suddenly, I come to an unfortunate realization. If I don't do this for her, if I don't act like a servant, then what am I really here for? What am I getting paid for? Well, I do help Jax out a lot. I serve him food and help him with his crutches. Take him outside. But now that our relationship has turned into something more interesting, will I still be doing that? Yes, of course. I decide. I'm here as a personal assistant. He's definitely not paying me to sleep with him. And we haven't even slept together yet. Perhaps, in the future...

My mind drifts again. I hate Opal for her snooty attitude and her self-importance. But there's also something else that I hate about her. I hate her for interrupting us. Our kiss. Now, instead of sitting around thinking about how wonderful our kiss was and how it could've become something more and what that could be, I'm sitting here thinking about Opal. Fuck her!

Slowly, I pick up one of her bags and unzip the top. I've never touched a Louis Vuitton bag before, and it's even nicer than I expected it to be. I love how soft and delicate the leather is. The structured frame of the bag reminds me of those vintage bags that everyone used to travel with in the movies from the 40s and 50s. If only my phone worked in this place, then I could actually look up how much one of these bags costs. Agh, why do you even bother, Sophia? I ask myself. It's Louis Vuitton; each one must cost a fortune. So the Grayson family is loaded, what else is new?

Inside Opal's bags, I find some gorgeous dresses, crop tops, designer jeans, and three smaller Louis Vuitton bags full of makeup. Once all the dresses are hung up in the closet and all the jeans and tops are folded nicely on the shelves, I check the bags for any leftover things that I might've forgotten. In the front pocket of the smallest bag, I find a box of pregnancy tests. I don't know what compels me, but I decide to count them. The box says that there should be ten, but she only has seven. Three are gone. Hmm. Why would three be gone?

I've never been in this situation, but my friend got pregnant in the eleventh grade. I remember standing next to her and holding her hand as we waited for the results of the first test. It was between third and fourth period. When the first test said that she was pregnant, she immediately took another one. That one confirmed the results of the first so she took another one and another one. We went through four tests before she finally gave up and believed that she was indeed pregnant.

I sit back down on the bed. I can't believe what I've discovered. Opal is pregnant. Or at least, she might be. Oh my God. I want to tell Jax, but I can't. Right? It's not my place. I was snooping through her stuff...Well, actually that's not true. She asked me to put everything away, and I made this discovery of the three missing tests inadvertently.

My mind continues to race. I don't know why I'm so involved with this. So what if Opal is pregnant? She's in her late twenties. It's not even that surprising. It's not like she's a teenager. It's not a big deal.

I try to remember whether she was wearing a ring of any sort when I saw her. Wedding ring? Engagement ring? No, the only ring that I saw on her hand was a small twist ring around her thumb. If that was anything sentimental, then it definitely wasn't from a significant other in her life.

But even if that was the case, who cares? She's in her late twenties, and she has every right to be pregnant even if she isn't married, or engaged, or with anyone. It's none of my business, and no matter how much I want to tell Jax, it's none of his business either. Damn it.

"Sophia! Sophia!" I hear Opal's voice traveling up the stairs.

Jesus Christ, I say to myself. I just met her a few minutes ago and she's already treating me like a servant.

"Yes?" I say, walking to the top of the stairs.

"Are you done yet?"

"Yes." I nod.

"Okay, great. Can you be a darling and get me some iced tea, please? I can't find Mr. Whitewater anywhere and I'm so thirsty. It's so fucking hot outside."

I stare at her.

"Sophia?" she asks and snaps her fingers. "Are you there?"

"Did you just snap at me?"

"Sorry, sorry, it's a dumb habit. I know we're not supposed to do that to the staff anymore. But who can keep up with all of these changes in socioeconomic relationships?"

Who the hell is this woman? And does she live on this planet?

"Sophia? Iced tea, please?" she says and walks away.

I sigh. I have to talk to her about this, but something tells me that it will be a very long and tedious conversation.

I go down to the kitchen and get the pitcher of iced tea from the refrigerator. I pour her a glass and bring it to her in the living room where Jax is still sitting on the couch.

"Here you go, Opal," I say.

"So how did you two meet?" she asks when I turn around to leave the room.

I don't know what to say.

"In a diner actually," Jax says after a moment.

"A diner, really?" Opal asks in her snooty, stuck up way. "That's weird."

"Why's that?" Jax challenges her.

"Just a step down from your typical fare, isn't it?"

"And what's that?" he asks. I'm on the verge of crying, and he's actually going to make her say it. Why is he doing this? Why are they both acting like I'm not here?

"Oh, I don't know." Opal tosses her hair. She opens her compact and fixes her perfect lipstick application. "Cocktail waitresses in five-star hotels? They aren't doing it for you anymore?"

"And what about you?"

"What about me?"

"Which tight end will it be this week, O? Or are you over football players in general now that a certain quarterback dumped you for a Victoria's Secret model?"

"Fuck you!" She turns to him. Jax wipes little droplets of spit off his face.

"Don't start something you don't want to finish, big sister. Or you'll be up way past your bedtime."

"Go fuck yourself, Jax." Opal gets up from her seat.

"Oh, what's the matter? You can dish it out, but you can't take it?" Jax yells at her.

"He was my fucking fiancé, Jax," she says. Her voice cracks a bit. Is she actually tearing up? No, that can't be it.

"I don't care." Jax shrugs, unfazed. "Sophia is my guest, and you're going to treat her with a little respect."

Opal gets a hold of her feelings and returns back to normal. "This is my house, too, and I'm going to treat the help any way I want to, bro."

Jax stood up for me. I'm grateful, but I also get the feeling that it made things a lot worse.

"Just so you know, we're not having dinner together tonight!" Jax yells after her, but she simply slams the door behind her.

"I don't think she was expecting to," I say.

"Fuck." Jax shakes his head. "I don't know why she has to be like that."

"Like what?" I joke.

"She's not always like this. Sometimes, she's nice. She can be really nice and kind. I don't know what the hell is going on with her, but ever since that son of a bitch dumped her, she's been a real bitch."

I find it hard to believe that Opal wasn't always a bitch, but I take his word for it.

"Listen, I'm sorry. I'm really sorry about her."

"It's okay," I sigh. I don't really know how else to respond to this whole situation. I've never been treated like this by complete strangers before. "I just feel like she hates me or something. For no good reason. Do you think she's jealous of me?"

Jax laughs. "No, I don't think so." His nonchalant laughter makes me tense up.

"Why are you laughing?" I ask.

"I don't know. Just the thought of O being jealous of you?"

"You're such a dick, Jax. You know that?" I shake my head and get up to leave.

"What? What did I say?"

I turn around to face him. The expression on his face is blank. He's either a total idiot or completely clueless.

"For your information, I didn't mean that O is jealous of me...I meant that she might be jealous of you and me. But you just had to take it somewhere shitty, didn't you? You know, I have a lot to offer. Just because you all have money and I don't have any doesn't mean that no one can be jealous of me. You fuckin' stuck up asshole."

I turn and walk out the door.

CHAPTER 24 - SOPHIA

WHEN HE APOLOGIZES...

I don't want to see his face again for a long time, but a few hours later, there's a knock at the door. I know who it is, but I don't answer.

"Go away."

"Sophia, please. I'm sorry. I didn't mean any of that. I don't know what came over me."

"I don't care. Go away," I say without getting off the bed. "How did you even get here with your casts on?"

I regret asking the question immediately. It just gives us something more to talk about. And that's the last thing I want right now.

"I had help,' Jax says. "I was just really mad at my

sister for how she was treating you. I don't know why she said any of those things."

"It's not her I'm mad at right now, Jax."

"I know. I know," he says and slaps the door with his hand. The slap is angry, but not at me. It sounds as if he's angry with himself. "Sophia, please open the door. I really want to apologize to you face-to-face. And then I'm going to go."

I take a moment, but eventually give in.

"What?" I ask, opening the door. My hands are folded across my chest. I am in no mood to hear anything but his most heartfelt apology.

"Sophia, I didn't mean any of that. I'm not going to make any excuses. That was wrong of me to say. It was wrong, and it was also untrue. I was an asshole. You know it. I know it. I'm sorry."

Wow. That was a much better apology than I'd expected. I thought he would make excuses, try to explain. I thought he would cloud up his apology with all the things that we usually say to diminish our wrongdoing. But he didn't.

I look at him. He's pressing both of his arms against the sides of the doorway and leaning into my room. But only slightly. He's no longer the cocky, arrogant Jax, who I've come to find so attractive.

There's another side to him. A vulnerable side. And I find this side is just as attractive.

"Okay." I nod.

"Okay?" His face lights up.

I nod again. I hate this part of the argument. That transition when one person apologizes and the other person accepts the apology. After that, there's this gap or space that forms between the two people. The space demands to be filled with some sort of bodily contact, but neither of us seems sure of who the first person should be to make the contact. He's the one who was wrong, the one who apologized, so I think it should be him. But looking at him and the way that his eyes are asking my permission, it seems like he thinks it should be me. Finally, I take a step forward.

That's enough of a lead for him to lean forward and take me into his arms.

"You know I can't stand your sister, right?" I say, pulling away from him.

"Yes, I know that." He presses his lips to mine.

"No, I don't think you do," I mumble. This time, I'm unable to pull away successfully. I struggle a little but eventually give in. His lips taste like strawberries, and his tongue dances with mine.

"How long is she staying here for?" I ask. I have
to ask now before things get more out of control.

"Can we not talk about my sister right now?" Jax
pulls at my tank top. "It's a little hard to get in
the mood."

"Really?" I laugh. "You seem to be having no
trouble." I nudge him a little, pointing at the hard
thing in his pants that's pushing into my stomach.

He laughs and continues to kiss me. He kisses
my neck and makes his way down to the top of my
breasts.

"How long will she be here for?" I ask again. I
need to have a date that I can look forward to.

"I don't know," he mumbles with his face buried
in my cleavage. "A few days. A week, maybe."

I nod. I try to believe him. I want to tell him that
it may be months because she might be pregnant.
Who the hell gets pregnant like that in this day and
age anyway? How stupid could she be? My mind
wanders again, but Jax's sloppy kisses bring me back
into this moment. Whatever I may know or not
know, I'm not going to tell him tonight. That would
ruin everything.

"Let's not talk about her anymore," I say.

"Good idea." He smiles.

Jax pushes me back against the wall and presses

his whole body against mine. He pulls on my hair slightly as he kisses my neck and my lips. The pressing and the pulling gives me goose bumps, and I feel myself getting wet. After a moment of high intensity, the kissing slows to a more measured pace. It's like our desperation for each other has vanished, if only for a moment, and we can really enjoy our time together.

But then Jax pulls away. His face has a very serious expression on it.

"What's wrong?"

"Nothing."

"Why did you stop?"

"I'm just not sure what all of this is going to do to our agreed upon friendship."

I don't even wait a second to answer. "Nothing. It's going to be good for it."

"Really? Are most friendships improved with jumping into bed together?" His lips are forming into a coy, little smile. I realize that he's joking. Making fun of me. Teasing me, even.

"What do you want me to say?" I ask.

"Nothing." He shakes his head. He's back to the cocky, arrogant guy I first laid my eyes on. "The ball's in your court."

CHAPTER 25 - SOPHIA

I don't want the ball. I want him to push me down and have his way with me. I want to just be taken over by feelings and pleasure without any of the responsibility of owning my feelings or decisions. Fuck! Fuck! Fuck!

"What are you going to do, Sophia?" Jax mocks me. "Are you going to ask me to stay a little longer? Or are you going to play by the rules?"

He's joking and making fun, but I know that his heart will be broken if I say I want to play by the rules. Stupid rules of friendship. Why did I put that in place anyway?

"And what if I asked you to leave?" I ask, licking my lips. He stares at them as if he can't look away.

"Then I'll leave," he says quietly.

"You promise?" I ask.

He cracks a smile. Who's going to give in first? I don't really care as long as it's someone.

"Please ask me to come in," he finally whispers.

I can't believe it. I've actually gotten him to do it.

"You're such a pushover." I laugh.

"No, not at all." He wraps his arms around me. "I just want you a lot."

Jax's lips are soft and irresistible. He holds me tight against his hard body. We struggle over to the bed. Once we lay down, his hands travel over my body, and I moan softly. There are no more rules to break – all of them have already been broken. No, all of them are about to be broken. And that's okay.

He strokes and kneads my thighs and they open up for him as if they were petals of a flower at sunrise. I get flushed with lust.

His hands pull my tank top over my head and allow my breasts to fall out. Jax grabs one with his hand and puts the other into his mouth. It feels like an electric current is running through me, making it impossible to concentrate on anything but this moment. Suddenly, the current focuses itself on the lower part of my body.

Jax's tongue starts to move its way down my body in endless circles. He sends me into a spiral of pleasure. I groan and buck against him. I move my hands down his rock hard body and discover that he's already naked. I'm not sure how or when he had taken them off. Maybe he never had them on. I'm happy to find him hard and straining for me.

I grip him and start to pump slowly. Jax's hands make their way past my clothes and inside of me and push me to the brink of the unknown. I wrap my legs around his body and push him inside of me.

It doesn't take either of us very long. A shuddering swell of sensation rises from somewhere deep within me. Jax starts to groan and I gasp. I throw my head back and a strong orgasm washes over me, rippling throughout my body and reaching its furthest extremes. With one last moan, Jax collapses on top of me.

The rest of the night passes in a blur. We stay up late eating junk food and laughing about every idiotic thing imaginable. He tells me stories of his brothers and how much they had as little kids, and I tell him funny stories of my own sister. I thought that having sex would change something for the worse. That's why I didn't want to do it originally. I thought it would make things odd and awkward, but instead I discovered that it only made things better.

"You know, I don't get you," I say. Jax is lying with

his head on my pelvis, and we're both staring at the ceiling.

"What don't you get?"

"Well, with other guys, my other boyfriends, they just rolled over and fell asleep almost immediately after."

"Agh, Sophia." He waves his hand in disgust. "I don't want to hear about other guys right now. Not after *that*."

"*That* was good. There's no denying that."

"Okay? So?"

"I was just trying to give you a compliment. All I wanted to say was that you're not like all of them."

"How's that?" Jax turns to me and props up his head with his hand.

"Well, we just had awesome sex, right?"

"Right."

"Awesome, mind-blowing sex?"

"Yes, I agree." He smiles.

"And you still want to talk to me afterward?"

"Who the hell have you been sleeping with that they didn't want to talk to you afterward?" he jokes. "Geez! And I thought I had bad taste in the opposite sex."

"No, no, no." I laugh. I love the easiness of our relationship. It's so easy to joke and laugh with him.

It's almost as if it's unreal. "It's not that they don't want to talk to me afterward…it's just different after sex. It's like the chase is over, and now they just want to relax."

"Well, I'm not like that." He kisses me.

"Yes, I can see that." I kiss him back.

"Besides, those guys are idiots."

"How so?"

"The chase is never over," he says confidently with his head tilted back. "What they don't take into account is that it doesn't just have to be a one-time thing. One night does not mean one time."

I look at him. His face is very serious and stern. Then with a little crack of the lips, a small smile starts to form, and I laugh out loud.

"Oh, I see. So you're taking the long view of things, are you?"

He comes close to me again. Jax leans into me. His fingers run along my jawline and bury themselves in my hair. He gets closer, and I feel his breath on my lips. But he doesn't kiss me on my lips. Instead, he demands that I wait. His kisses me on my upper lip then my lower lip. He leans down and runs his lips over my neck – quietly, smoothly, gently. It's as if it were our first kiss. Gentle. Memorable.

"The long view is all there is," he whispers. "And the night's still young."

I bury my hands in his hair and pull his head up to mine. I have to taste him. I have to touch his tongue with mine. When our lips meet, shivers spread through my body. His tongue feels rough and strong. He grabs my face and kisses me more passionately with each breath. It is no longer gentle or sweet. Now, he is kissing me as if he were trying to prove something. In this kiss, there is longing and hope. He devours me, and I devour him.

Suddenly, he pulls away. I am just about to say something, but he puts his index finger to his lips and pulls down both straps of my shirt. He lets them dangle there for a moment. Then he leans down and exposes my breast and places it carefully in his mouth. Again, he is gentle at first, carefully licking me and playing with them. My knees go weak. But Jax's kisses only intensify. He grabs my other breast, toeing the line between pleasure and pain.

I'm getting wetter and wetter. My hands feel rushed, shaking in anticipation, but he pushes them away. He doesn't give in. Instead, he lifts my top over my head and lets my breasts bounce into his mouth. Carefully, he wraps his mouth around me, taking almost all of it inside. I run my fingers through his luscious hair and try to pull up his head to face me. But he doesn't give in. He continues to suck on my nipples, spreading his time evenly between both breasts.

He pushes aside my panties, smiling at how soaking wet they are and spreads me open. He runs his fingers over my pussy, not going inside. He continues to tease me, giving me little butterfly kisses from my navel to my thighs and yet avoiding the one area that I want to feel his lips.

I lean back on the bed, enjoying the moment, and craving what would come next.

As if he were reading my mind, he grabs the side of my panties with his teeth and starts tugging at them. I wiggle my body to help them along, enjoying the ferociousness of his actions.

I can see that his games are trying for both of us. I finally reach down and grab his large erect cock. It pulsates and throbs in my hand. Two can play at this game.

I run my fingers over him, accentuating every line and curve. His eyes roll to the back of his head for a moment. Then he comes back. I try to grab him again; I want to put him in my mouth, but he doesn't let me.

Instead, he pushes my legs and opens me up. His

fingers go deep inside of me, and his tongue makes swirls over and over until I scream his name. He licks hard and then goes deep in large concentric circles that condense into smaller ones. His fingers dig deep inside and dance to a silent melody that only he can hear.

My hips start to move up and down uncontrollably. I am getting close. A moment later, my legs grow numb, my toes dig into the bed, and a warm, soothing sensation spreads throughout my body. A waterfall of pleasure covers me from head to toe.

CHAPTER 26 - JAX

*S*ophia is the sweetest thing I've ever tasted. I don't know who those idiots were that fell asleep immediately after having sex with her, but all I want to do is stay up and worship her all night. I can't believe that I'm lucky enough to be with her. It is almost five o'clock when we finally fall asleep in each other's arms after a long night of lovemaking. I thought I was in shape, but my whole body is sore all over.

The following morning, I wake up and notice that it's almost noon. Sophia is nowhere to be found, but comes back after I get dressed.

"I made you some breakfast," she says, carrying a tray with waffles, pancakes, and fresh fruit. "I would've loved to go out and gotten some bagels and some store bought coffee, but this will have to do."

I wobble to her and kiss her on the mouth.

"Okay, okay." She quiets me down. "Let's at least have breakfast first."

I sit down on the bed next to her. Man, am I hungry. I grab the top waffle and shove it in my mouth.

"Last night was amazing," I say. "I had an awesome time."

"Me, too," she says with a wide smile. She is freshly showered and smells of lavender and honey. Her hair glistens in the sunlight.

"What do you want to do today?" she asks.

"You mean besides spend the whole day with you in bed?"

"Yes, besides that." She chuckles.

"I want to go outside. See the horses. Say hi to Sebastian," I say without a moment's hesitation.

The expression on her face changes immediately.

"What do you mean?"

"Nothing, don't worry. I'm not going to ride him."

"I hope not," she says. But the gravity does not vanish from her face.

I put my arm around her. "What's wrong?"

"Nothing. You just scared me," she says.

I don't understand. Then it hits me. "Just by mentioning the horses?"

She nods.

"It's going to be okay. It was just an accident. Sebastian's a good horse. He's sweet, you'll see. And the others. Well, they haven't done anything at all."

Sophia shakes her head. "I just don't want anything to happen to you."

"I know. And it won't." I kiss her on the top of her head.

"You promise?" She looks up at me with those big wide brown eyes. They are impossible to say no to.

"Yes, I promise," I say.

***

SOPHIA and I get ready to go out and see the horses. After interrupting her in her process of getting dressed and pulling her back into bed, we finally get it together enough to exit the bedroom.

"Mr. Grayson?" Mr. Whitewater says, standing right outside the door.

"Oh my God, you nearly gave me a heart attack!" Sophia jumps back into me.

"I'm terribly sorry, I didn't mean to startle you," Mr. Whitewater apologizes. "But there's a woman downstairs who's asking for you. Are you expecting anyone, Mr. Grayson?"

I shrug, shaking my head. "Sophia?"

She shakes her head no.

Mr. Whitewater explains. "The woman downstairs is claiming to be your mother."

"Mom? Mom?" Sophia rushes past him and runs down the stairs. "Mom?"

From the top of the stairs, I see a woman dressed in a blue suit and a matching wide-brimmed hat standing in the foyer.

"Mom, what are you doing here?" Sophia asks. "Is everything okay?"

"Yes, of course!" Sophia's mom hugs her. She then gives her a peck on each cheek, careful not to smudge her makeup.

"Jax, this is my mom," Sophia says without actually giving me a name. "Mom, this is Jax."

"It's a pleasure to meet you, Ms. Cole." I shake her hand. Her hand is warm and firm, and her whole way of occupying the room reminds me of one of my favorite aunts.

"Oh, please call me Danielle."

"Danielle," I repeat the name to burn it into my memory. "It's so wonderful to finally meet you. Sophia, why didn't you tell me that your mother looks like she could be your sister?"

Both Sophia and Danielle blush. Women always do when I say something like that to them. The only difference in this statement is that I actually mean it. Danielle looks so young and full of life that an unsuspecting stranger could actually confuse her for Sophia's sister.

"What a beautiful home you have here Jax." Danielle walks around the foyer. She carries herself with a familiar strength and confidence that reminds me of my mother and sister, but the likes of which I've rarely seen in strangers entering the house.

"This vase, it's absolutely marvelous!" Danielle points to one of my mother's favorite vases standing tall on a side table. Its history stems back all the way to the seventeenth century.

"You've got an excellent eye, Danielle," I say. "It used to belong to my great-great-great-grandmother who came from Virginia."

Suddenly, I notice the strange expression on Sophia's face.

"Mom? What are you talking about?" she whispers.

"What's wrong?" I ask. Danielle walks to the other side of the room where I doubt she can hear us.

"I don't know who this woman is," Sophia whispers to me.

"What are you talking about? Isn't this your mom?"

"Yes, of course! But it's also not her. I don't know. I don't know why she's dressed like that. Or how she knows about seventeenth century vases."

"I know about seventeenth century vases because I watch a healthy amount of *Antiques Roadshow*," Danielle says. She either has excellent hearing or must not have been far enough away to be out of our earshot. Sophia blushes.

"Mom? Can I talk to you, in private?" Sophia asks.

"No, Sophia. That would be rude." Danielle waves her hand in a casual manner that I've often seen my mother and her rich girlfriends do to their servants.

I feel the tension between them building, at least on Sophia's side, and step in to broker peace.

"Ms. Cole, I mean, Danielle, would you like to join us for lunch? My sister's visiting us as well, and I know she'd love to meet you."

Danielle quickly agrees, and I excuse myself to make arrangements.

AFTER WE HAVE LUNCH...

*A*n hour later, we all sit down for lunch – Sophia, Danielle, O, and I. This was not the way that I'd planned the day to go. The last thing I want to do is spend more time with O, who still hasn't apologized for her rude behavior. And who I have yet to forgive. But the presence of Sophia's mother at lunch is quite interesting. I've never met this woman, whose life I saved, or rather my money has saved, and a big part of me is eager to get to know her more.

Danielle makes herself comfortable at the head of the table and talks almost non-stop about how well she's doing and about her new fiancé.

"Luke and I have been practically living together

for these last two months," she says with an
exuberant flair that reminds me of O.

"Luke?" Sophia asks.

"Yes, Luke. Remember, I told you about him?"

"Yes, you told me that you were seeing a guy
named Luke, but you haven't really mentioned him
for a month."

Sophia is steaming. Anger is bubbling up from
some dark place within her.

"Tell me more about Luke, Danielle. What's he
like?" O pipes in. She can't help herself, can she?
What I can't figure out is why is she doing this? Is
she doing this because she hates Sophia? Or just for
fun? And what reason can she possibly have to hate
Sophia?

"Oh, my darling, Opal. Luke is fabulous! He's
Swiss, and he lives in France. He's got plenty of
money, and he wants me to move to France with him
as soon as possible after the wedding."

"What are you talking about, Mom?" Sophia's
face grows pale. "You've just met him! And now
you're moving to France?"

"Sophia, I know that this seems sudden. But
Luke and I are in love. I know that I might seem a bit
different to you—"

"A bit different?" Sophia gasps. "It's like you

morphed into some rich, stuck up princess overnight."

"Now, there's no need to be rude."

"Yes, yes, there is, mother," Sophia says. She uses the word mother in a derogatory way, the way preteen girls on television usually say it. "It's like you've lost your mind or something!"

Danielle shakes her head and looks away.

"So how did you meet your Luke?" O asks. At this moment, I'm thankful that O is here with us. The tension between Sophia and her mom is growing, and I'm pretty certain that it will result in an explosion. The only thing I'm not sure about is whether I can stop it.

"Online. We met up in downtown LA and have been inseparable since."

Sophia shakes her head. She's about to say something, but I put my hand on her knee to stop her.

"It's okay," I whisper. "It's going to be okay."

Somehow, we make it through the rest of lunch. I manage to calm Sophia down and give space for O to connect with Danielle. By the end of lunch, they seem inseparable. They are laughing at each other's corny jokes. I've never seen O act this way with anyone else except for her close friends and never

our own mother. It's as if Danielle is the mother that
O never had.

***

"I DON'T KNOW who that person is in there," Sophia
says to me when we are finally alone in my bedroom.
O is showing Danielle around the gardens, and I sneak
away with Sophia. It gives her some breathing room.

"What are you talking about?"

"That woman is not my mother," Sophia says,
sitting down on the bed. She buries her hands in her
hair. I try to rub the back of her neck, but she pushes
me away.

"It's going to be okay," I say. "She seems perfectly
lovely."

"You don't fuckin' get it, do you, Jax? She's not my
mother. She looks like her and sounds like her, but
it's not her."

"What are you talking about?"

"I don't know what this Luke wants, but he wants
something."

"What could he want?"

"Something. Why else would he be with her?"

That hurts my feelings. She doesn't even know what she's saying, but her words cut deep.

"I don't want anything. And I'm with you," I say and turn away from her.

"That's not what I meant," she whispers. She approaches me and wraps her hands around my shoulders, but this time it is me who brushes her away.

"You think that I want something from you?" I ask. Looking far into the horizon, I see Danielle and O laughing by the rose bushes.

"No, that's not what I meant. But then again..."

She lets her words trail off. I wait for her to explain. Finally, she does.

"But then again, I am here because you requested my presence here."

"Do you want to leave?"

"No, not anymore. But I did originally come here to pay off a debt."

"Fuck you, Sophia. Everything I did for you and your mom was because I wanted to. I asked you to come. I asked you. I didn't demand you to. You could've come or not. And you can leave at any time."

I turn around to walk toward the door. She catches up with me.

"Jax, please. I'm sorry."

But I'm not in the mood to forgive.

"You can go anytime," I say and head for the door. Before I get there, she stops me. She forces me to turn around. I didn't know that she was so strong. She pushes herself up to my lips and presses hers onto mine.

Something comes over me. I'm mad at her; I don't want to kiss her. But I do. I get erect as she rubs it, and she unbuckles my jeans and lets them fall to the floor. We kiss as if the world is going to end in a minute and rip our clothes off with the same ferocity.

I want her.

I need her.

She wants me.

She has to have me.

My shirt falls to the floor. Her shirt lands on top. I undo her bra and grab her breasts with my hands. She moans from pleasure. I rip off her panties and step out of my briefs.

She buries her fingers in my hair and kisses the back of my neck. She lets her hands slide down my washboard abs and squeezes me. I wince from the mixture of pain and pleasure.

With one quick motion, I toss her on the bed and spread open her legs. Within another second, I'm in her again. I pull in and out, and pleasure builds within my thighs.

"Oh, Jax," she moans as I pull gently on her hair. Her moans get louder and more powerful. I'm getting closer, too.

A few more thrusts and I collapse on top of her. Satisfied. From the smile on her face, I know she is, too.

"Thank you," she says.

"No, thank you."

CHAPTER 28 - JAX

AFTER THERE'S A STALEMATE...

*a*fter sex, I try not to talk about her mother anymore, but that's the only thing that is on Sophia's mind.

"I just don't know why she's acting like this. Why she's dressed like that? Why she's hanging out with Opal? Do you think she's having some sort of mental breakdown?" she rants.

I'm only half listening. I'm sleepy and tired, and all I want to do is turn over and go to sleep. But I nod along and try to be supportive. I don't know much about women, but what I do know is that they want their men to be supportive. And being supportive means listening along to their rants and nodding in agreement.

"So?" Sophia stops talking. I open my eyes and look around the room. She's already fully dressed in the same thing she was wearing only an hour ago.

"So what?" I ask.

"What do you think?"

"I don't know, Sophia." I shrug. I already told her what I thought, and she didn't want to hear it.

"I really want to know."

"I already told you what I thought," I say. I'm trying to avoid actually saying the words, but all signs are pointing to the fact that this might be inevitable.

"I want to hear it again. If it's still what you think," she says cautiously. She's no longer ranting. If I do this, I'm going to have to proceed with caution.

"I don't know your mother, Sophia, but the woman I met today seemed fine to me. She seemed happy. Maybe she seems so different to you because she's actually happy for once. She's no longer worried about her cancer or dying. Maybe she's just trying to live her life to the fullest."

Sophia doesn't say anything. I wait for her to process what I've said. Her face remains expressionless, and, after a while, I start to get worried that this was the wrong way to proceed.

She's not getting this. She's not in agreement, and we're going to get into another big fight. But then she surprises me.

"Maybe you're right." She shrugs. "I'm going to go downstairs and talk to her."

———————

THAT NIGHT AT DINNER, things between Sophia and Danielle are at a stalemate. Sophia spoke with her mother in private, and I don't know what was said. All I know is that somehow things got worse. They are no longer fighting, but just ignoring each other.

Danielle was planning on leaving before dinner, but O, of course, got in the middle of it all and insisted that she stay.

"You can't leave now, you just got here. Please stay for dinner. You must stay for dinner!" she said, grabbing her arm. Much to my and Sophia's dismay, Danielle agreed.

Dinner becomes divided into two camps. Sophia only speaks to me and Danielle only speaks to O. O doesn't bother to speak to Sophia, who I'm now convinced that she hates wholeheartedly, but she does speak to me. Sophia doesn't speak to O nor her mother. I try to speak to both O and Danielle, but when I do, Sophia ignores me and stares at her plate.

Awful. Shitty. Ridiculous. All words that come to mind to describe this dinner, one of the worst ones of my life.

Finally, when the dessert comes, I see the light at the end of the tunnel. It's almost over, I say to myself. You just gotta hang in there for half an hour more. Forty-five max.

"Ahem." Danielle stands up and raises her glass. "I'd like to make a toast."

O leans forward in her seat, exhibiting the eagerness of a first grader on her first day of school. Sophia, on the other hand, shrinks in her seat as if she wants to disappear.

"I would like to thank you, Opal, for being such a wonderful hostess. I know that I came without much of an announcement, but meeting you has been quite a treat."

"No, please." O blushes. "It has been my pleasure."

"I would also like to thank you, Sophia. You aren't as excited about me being here as I thought you would be, but nevertheless, it has been wonderful to see you again. I've really missed you, honey."

I look closer and there are small tears pooling at the bottom of her eyes. Sophia looks at her, too.

"Thanks for coming," she manages, which seems to be enough for her mom, who smiles widely.

"And finally, I would like to thank you, Jax."

That's unexpected.

"Thank me? For what?"

"For everything, of course. For my life. The money that you gave us. No, that you gave Sophia for my treatments. It has been a lifesaver in the truest sense."

"What money?" O perks up.

"Oh, you know, the money that Jax gave me to pay for cancer treatments. Our insurance company refused to pay for the experimental treatment and, if it weren't for that money, I'd be dead right now."

I shake my head.

"No, I'm serious, Jax. I would be. You saved my life. And of course, I have to go back and thank my little Sophia for taking care of me during all of those years, and for finally getting out of the house, so that I had some space to date and find myself a man."

"Mom." Sophia shakes her head. But Danielle ignores her.

"I'm terribly sorry that my daughter is acting like

this," she says to Opal and me. "I've taught her to behave better than this, that's for sure."

"Oh, really? Is that what you did, mother? And when was that? When I gave up my future to stay home and work at some shitty diner to take care of you when you were dying of cancer? Or when I came here to pay off the debt for *your* cancer treatments?"

How did this nice toast suddenly get so out of hand?

"Debt? What debt?" O turns to me. "What is she talking about, Jax?"

She finally got it. I can't believe it took her this long. But then again, she's always been a bit slow.

Damn.

Fuck.

Shit.

How the fuck did this come out? Why didn't Sophia keep her mouth shut?

"Nothing, no debt," I mumble. My mind races to find just the right excuse that makes sense to this story.

"I don't know what you're talking about."

No one says anything for a few moments.

"I don't understand," O says. "How much money did you give them exactly?"

"Not much." I shrug.

"Oh my God, no! It was a lot, O," Danielle insists. Fuck her. Fuck her!! I want to scream.

"But how much exactly?" O asks.

"You didn't tell her?" Danielle turns to me. "You were so generous and you didn't brag about it? O, it was $250,000. Can you believe that? It was more money than I've ever seen. And your wonderful brother, he just wrote Sophia a check after meeting her only a few times. His heart is so big."

I can see the anger building within O. She purses her lips. Narrows her eyes. "That's definitely one way of putting it."

"What? Whatever you're going to say, just say it already, O. Come on out with it." I can't stand this anymore.

"Oh, you want me to just say it? Okay. Fine. What about me?"

"What about you?"

"You knew that I needed money. That mom and dad cut me off. And instead, you just chose to give that money away to strangers. How could you?"

"They needed it for something better, O. All you would do is go shopping and party."

"Fuck you, Jax! I'm your sister. Who cares what the hell some strangers in a diner need the money for? That's their problem. This money, it's our money. Our family's money. And you had no right to give it away just to get some pussy."

"That's not why I did it."

"I don't care!!" O is hysterical. She's walking around, pacing, screaming. I'm keeping my distance. I feel like she's going to explode at any minute.

CHAPTER 29 - JAX

AFTER THE FIGHT…

O and I continue to scream at each other. It's like we're children again. Nothing matters now, but to yell at each other. Whoever says the meanest, loudest thing wins. Wins what, though? Neither of us knows.

"I can't believe you did this for her!" O's face is flushed. She feels like she's losing. I know because she always starts to bring other people into the fight when she feels like she's losing ground.

"What's wrong with her?" I ask. "She's perfect."

I say it. I mean it. I glance over at Sophia. She smiles.

"She's white trash!" O screams. "Trash! Trash!"

"Fuck you, Opal!" Sophia pipes in. I don't want her to be a part of this, but she already is.

"Who the hell do you think you're calling trash?"

"You, you bitch!"

O puts her hands on her hips. She thinks she's gaining ground. Her attention is diverted to someone weaker. Someone without a strong position. Or so she thinks. I look over at Sophia. Her face is expressionless. Her eyes are unflinching. It's like she has something on O. She knows something she shouldn't.

"At least I'm not the one who's pregnant. And unmarried. Single. Am I right, Opal?"

Pregnant! What the hell is she talking about? O's not pregnant.

"What's she talking about, O?"

I wait for O to fight back. Tell Sophia to shut up, send her to hell. But she doesn't. Instead, she breaks down. Her legs buckle under her and she drops to the floor.

"O!" I go to her and wrap my arms around her. I've never seen O this fragile. At least, not since her boyfriend killed himself the day before their prom.

"What the fuck are you talking about, Sophia?"

"It's true." She shrugs. I hate how cold she is. A few moments ago, I felt nothing but love and warmth for her. But now, all that's gone.

"It's true," Sophia insists. "Isn't it, O?"

I've never heard her call O that, and I hate the way she says it.

"O?" I ask. Her face is buried in my shoulders. She's sobbing.

"Yes," she mumbles. "I think so."

I continue to hold her. Sophia stares at me. Something in her eyes tells me that she's sorry. I pull away from O and she stands up on her own two feet.

"Tell me what happened."

"He left. He left me," she sobs. "And your girlfriend has no right to go through my bags!"

"Yes, I do! You were the one who told me to put all your shit away because you're such a princess that you couldn't do it yourself."

"Sophia, please," I say.

"You're telling me to be quiet?" Sophia gasps.

"Yes, I am. Can't you see that O's having a difficult time here?"

"I can't believe you're taking her side!"

"I'm not taking anyone's side. There are no sides. There's just this crazy situation that I just heard about," I say.

I turn to O. "How did this happen? Why?"

But she doesn't say a word. Instead, she sobs and buries her face in her hands. I fuckin' knew it. I knew it. O's ex, if you can call him that, was such an asshole. He was a ruthless playboy that cheated on her incessantly and told her he loved her.

"I just don't understand what you saw in him, O. He was such a dick."

She shrugs and continues to cry.

The three of us stand in a semi-circle, unsure as to what to do. Danielle sits motionless at the table.

Finally, I turn to Sophia.

"How long did you know?" I ask.

"Ever since I unpacked her bags the other day. I was going to keep this private, but..."

"You had no right to keep it private," I say. I don't know why I said that. When Sophia's eyes grow big with astonishment and shock, I want to take those words back immediately, but I can't.

"What are you talking about?" Sophia crosses her arms across her chest.

"Nothing." I shrug.

"This wasn't even her news to reveal! You bitch," O hisses.

"Okay, I've had enough of this." Sophia throws her hands up and turns to leave the room.

"Where are you going, darling?" Danielle walks after her.

"I need to get out of here."

Danielle follows her out, leaving O and me alone

in the room. I turn to her. I don't know what to say. I want to yell at her for being so stupid. How could she just get pregnant like this with that moron's baby? And is she planning on keeping it? What will our parents say?

But she looks at me with her large puppy dog eyes, and I can't do any of those things. All I see is my sister and that she's lost. Alone. Scared. Terrified, probably. I would be, and I wouldn't even be the one who's pregnant.

"Are you okay?" I ask quietly. "Can I get you something?"

She shakes her head no. She sits back down. I look her over, up and down. I look for signs of pregnancy, but there are none. Except that she didn't drink this evening. Strange. I didn't notice that before.

"I hate that girl," she says. I sigh.

"You two just got off to a bad start. You came in here ordering her around. What did you think was going to happen?"

"I thought she was the fuckin' help, Jax. How was I supposed to know that she's your girlfriend? You said that she worked here."

"She does. But that's not all she is. I don't know. It's complicated."

She smiles. I don't remember the last time I saw that beautiful smile. It puts me at ease.

"Tell me about it," she says, rubbing her non-existent belly.

I ask her about the father. At first, she doesn't want to talk, but eventually she caves. They have been on and off for two years. This happened during one of the on-times.

"At least he's got money," I say.

She shrugs. "I don't care about the money."

I look around the room. Frantically, as if I'm searching for something.

"What's wrong?" she asks.

"I'm just looking for my sister. Because this girl in front of me who said that she doesn't care about money, that can't possibly be my sister."

"Oh, shut up." O laughs. I'm glad that I'm still able to make her laugh. "I've grown up. I'm going to be a mom."

"So I heard."

"She had no right to tell you. That's why I got so mad at her. That and my hormones are all out of whack now."

"I know." I nod. "But she did. So what? Do you want me to keep your secret for you?"

CHAPTER 30 - JAX

WHEN SHE LEAVES...

"Yes." She nods. "I just can't tell anyone else yet. I can't have Mom and Dad finding out. Not before I decide what to do about all this."

"Oh, so you're not decided?" I ask.

"Don't get so excited. I'm pretty sure I'm going to keep it. I just need some time. I'm not sure how to break it to them quite yet. I need time."

I nod. I understand. Mom and Dad are difficult people to break things to. They have so many standards and rules. Plus, they are way too easily disappointed by their children. Whenever you present them with a new idea, it's very important to have an answer for everything. And with this whole situation, they will eat her alive.

"Will you help me?" O asks. "Help me come up with a plan?"

I smile and nod. Not sure what kind of plan we can come up with, but some sort of plan would be better than nothing. I know that for sure.

"You owe me," she adds.

"Owe you for what?"

"For giving away a quarter of a million dollars to some stranger." The tone of her voice shows that she's joking, but not really.

"It was for a good cause."

"Oh, please." O rolls her eyes. "Good cause, my ass. If that had been some guy with a humpback and his mother was dying, you wouldn't give two shits about them."

I roll my eyes. Shrug. Shake my head no. But we both know that she's right.

"Just tell me one thing, okay?"

"What?"

"Why her? What's so special about her?"

I think about it for a moment. I want to say it's because she's the most beautiful girl I've ever seen. Or the funniest. Or the wittiest. But none of those things are true.

"She was the only one who said no. A couple of times, too. And then, I just had to have her."

O throws her head back and laughs. "You guys are all the same."

I nod in agreement. Perhaps, we are.

"Okay, so? Now that you had her? Was she worth it?"

"Yes," I say immediately. "Yes, she was." I would say that to O anyway, even if Sophia wasn't worth it, but it's not a lie. Everything in my body says that I'm right. That what we have has been right and good and perfect.

"So now that you know the truth, that Sophia and I are the real thing, you're going to have to treat her a little better. A lot better."

O laughs and rolls her eyes, but agrees.

Before leaving, Sophia's mother stops by to bid us goodbye. I'm not sad to have her go, but I'm surprised that she's leaving so soon. I invite her to stay half-heartedly, but she insists that she must go. Luke is waiting for her. She has a plane to catch out of LAX. Our goodbye is short. She thanks me again for the money and shakes my hand. She congratulates O on her pregnancy, tells her to not worry and call her at any time if she has any concerns. O agrees and, by the tone of her voice, I know that she actually might. It's odd how well O and Danielle connected. O isn't one to make friends easily with other women. The closeness that I see between them reminds me of how far apart O is from our own mother. But then again, relationships between mothers and daughters are often difficult and treacherous. My mother barely spoke two words to my grandmother, and I have hardly anything to say to my father.

"What about Sophia? Should I call her down?" I ask.

"Oh, no, there's no need. We already said our goodbyes. It was a pleasure to meet you both."

———

AFTER DANIELLE LEAVES, I go upstairs to see Sophia. Something doesn't feel right. I call her name going up the stairs, but she doesn't reply. I say it again when I knock on her door. But again I hear nothing.

"Sophia?" I ask, opening the door. "Are you okay? Your mom just left."

Her bags lay open on her bed. They are half full of clothes and she sits on her bed facing the window. She doesn't turn around, but as I get closer, I can see that she has been crying. Her eyes are puffy. Her makeup is smeared and her cheeks are red.

"What's wrong? Are you okay?"

She shakes her head no. She opens her mouth to say something but gets choked up by her tears.

"Why are your bags out? Where are you going?"

She takes a moment to gather herself. She stands up and wipes away her tears. "I'm leaving," she says.

"What?!" All the air gets knocked out of me.

"I'm leaving," she repeats herself quietly. "I can't stay here anymore."

"But why?"

"Opal's pregnant. And now that you know, she needs you. My mom is going to be in France for a while, so I'm going back home. You don't need me here."

I don't understand anything she's saying. "What does any of this, of us, have to do with O?"

"What does it have to do with O?" she yells. "Everything! She doesn't want me here. She hates me. She wants me gone. And now that she's going to stay here, I'm going to leave." She breaks down as she yells, but then gathers her thoughts and continues, "Okay, listen. I'm sorry about yelling. But O is pregnant. And she needs you. And she wants me out."

"I don't care what O wants." I shake my head. No, this can't be happening.

"But I do. She's going to stay here, in her house. And I don't need to be here."

I search my mind for things I can say to make her stay.

"What about the debt?" I finally ask. I don't want to bring it up, but nothing else comes to mind.

"What about it?" Sophia crosses her arms across her chest.

"We have an arrangement here. Don't we?"

"Oh, is that what this is about? You think that whatever job I was doing here is worth a quarter of a million dollars a year?"

"Yes," I lie.

"Well, in that case, I'm just going to get a real job and pay you back every cent from that."

"That's the last thing I want. You know that," I say. "And that's going to take forever, anyway."

Sophia walks over to the closet and starts throwing clothes into her suitcase.

"How about this? Why don't you just hire someone a little more compatible with your sister to be your servant around here? I bet she'll like that."

"Of course, she will!" I close the suitcase. I try to stop her from packing like a little child. I'm pathetic and stupid, and it's all I can be right now. "But this, this thing between us, it has nothing to do with her. I thought that you liked being here. Liked spending time with me. Was I wrong?"

Sophia sighs deeply. "No, you weren't."

"So why are you leaving?"

"Because it's all getting to be too much. It's not just us here anymore. And I need some time to think about everything that has happened."

I know there's nothing else I can say or do to change her mind. I'm not here to keep her hostage. If she wants to leave, she has every right to. No matter how much it hurts me. In silence, I watch her pack her bag. She's no longer tossing things into it mindlessly, she's folding each piece. Her mind is made up. All I can do now is let her go and see if she comes back to me.

CHAPTER 31 - SOPHIA

WHEN I SAY GOODBYE...

Two weeks later, the shorter days of the approaching winter descend upon my mom's trailer, wrapping it in a dark cloud. In the past, this place was my space to be myself. It infused me with hope and made me feel as if everything was going to be okay. But not anymore.

I came back home to get back something I felt like I lost. My sense of myself. But this place is no longer my space for solace. It isn't home.

As I look around these two rooms, everything is in its place. The pots and pans are in the bottom cupboard next to the stove. The plates are on the lower shelf near the stove. All utensils are in the broken drawer next to the sink. Mom had cleaned this place before she left, and it is the cleanest I've ever seen it. But that isn't why everything feels different.

Mom's not here anymore, I remember saying to myself. This place is all mine for a while. It's okay to make it my own.

But these words rang hollow. The person who came back here is a stranger. Her mother is now marrying some rich Swiss guy whom she's never met. She is falling in love with a spoiled billionaire who is a little too used to buying everything he ever wanted. And beyond all that, she, Sophia Cole, is also a stranger. She doesn't know who she is. She doesn't know what she is meant to do here. She doesn't know why she left or why she came back home.

Leaving that night was the hardest thing I've ever had to do. I have been sitting around my mom's trailer for days now, doing nothing, and feeling no better about what has happened. Thinking back now, I don't even know what the hell propelled me to leave. On one hand, it was Opal. Her cruelty and attitude and hatred for everything that I was. But, on the other hand, it was more than just Opal.

It was my mom's sudden announcement and her ability to just move on with her life. I've never seen my mom act that way. For as long as I've ever known her, she has been dwelling and living in the past. It's as if the present didn't exist. All that existed was her life back then, even before her cancer diagnosis... when my sister was still alive. I've spent years trying to get her to move on with her life. To embrace what life has to offer. And now that she has, finally, I don't know what to do with myself. I'm angry at her. I'm pissed off. How dare she move on? How dare she be happy?

Agh, what a petulant and spoiled brat I am. I hate myself for these thoughts, and yet it is beyond me to make them stop. They're like a streaming video that I can't turn off. They simply come without an invitation and continue until they are done.

When I finally do get a quiet second, my thoughts turn to other things. Jax.

Why did I run out on him like that? Because of Opal, but she wasn't the only reason. She was only a pretense.

I'm also angry. I started to pack my bags for one reason. I was angry with my mom, and I wanted to stop her. I wanted to beg her to stay. But then, when I'd realized that that was impossible, I needed to keep going. My anger at her morphed into something else completely. It became anger at Opal and, eventually, anger with Jax. Why didn't he defend me more to Opal? Why didn't he take my side? I didn't care that I was wrong. That I acted like a child, telling everyone the secret that I had no right to tell anyone.

I could've used that secret to connect with O. I could've told just her and I could've opened myself up to be her confidant. I could've kept her secret, and she would've thanked me for it. But instead, I did something else. I acted like a brat. I thought that he would be mad at her, but why would he be? She's his sister, and he loves her. He wants her in his life. He's going to be there for her.

"Fuck you, Jax," I mutter. It has been more than two weeks since I left, but my anger at him and myself has only multiplied. "No, fuck you, Sophia."

I'm hungrier than usual. I open the refrigerator and eat a cold slice of last night's pizza. Nothing too nutritious can satisfy my hunger now.

That fateful night when I decided to leave runs over and over in my head. And then an unexpected thought hits me.

I'm afraid.

There. I finally thought those words out loud. The next step is to say it out loud.

"I'm afraid. I was afraid," I say. But of what? Of being happy. Of fighting for what I wanted. For staying with Jax and seeing where our relationship could go.

"And what relationship is that?" I'm now talking to myself. "You had sex a few times, so what? That hardly constitutes a relationship. Lots of people have sex without much of a relationship. I'm sure that Jax has had sex plenty without being in any relationship."

I say those words out loud, partly because I feel like I have to and partly because I want to make them true. But they aren't. We didn't label it or define it, but what Jax and I had, had been a relationship. At least the beginning of one. And that was worth a lot. To both him and me.

"And I ruined it," I whisper.

CHAPTER 32 - SOPHIA

*A*nother two weeks pass without one incident. I see that I've fallen into darkness, engulfed with boredom, but I can't do anything about it to change it. The world outside is sunny and sparkly. The sky is bright blue without a single cloud, but it doesn't bring me any happiness. I know I need to get up off the couch and go outside, at least for a walk, but I don't have the energy. All I can muster myself up to do all day is to dial to get some food delivered. Even going to the grocery store seems like a task that's too big to conquer.

This has to stop, I say to myself. I need to get a job. At least my old one. Then I can start thinking of what else to do with my life. But instead, I just pick up my phone and read the gossip magazines.

Cellulite and how to lose ten pounds are the most important problems in the issues, and I'm terrified of stepping on the scale. I feel like I have gained at least ten pounds, if not more, in the last month.

Wait a second. Has it been a month already?

Suddenly, I'm filled with energy. I run over to the kitchen and leaf through the old calendar. It's three months off, but the year is correct.

"Shit. Shit. Shit."

My hands grow cold and my fingers get numb. I touch my neck and it feels like a stranger is touching me. I shudder and zip my hoodie.

"No, this can't be. No. No. No."

I shake my head. But it definitely can. I grab the keys to the car. On the way to the pharmacy, I pray that it's not true.

"Please, please, don't let this be true. This has to be a mistake. We just did it a few times. This can't be happening."

I turn up the radio to drown out my thoughts, but they refuse to go away. It wasn't just one time. It was twice. And both times, we didn't use any protection. Why? How could I have been so stupid??

I've never had sex with anyone without protection before. What if he has some sort of disease? What if I have it now?

But a mysterious illness is not the most important thing on my mind.

When was the last time I had my period? I try to remember. I count the days, but I can't quite remember. All I know is that it definitely wasn't this month.

Fuck!! I scream and shake myself, grabbing onto the steering wheel.

"No, no, no. This isn't happening," I whisper to myself. I try to calm myself down, but nothing works.

———

I GET home from the pharmacy in a daze. There were like a million different pregnancy test brands at the pharmacy. How the hell are you supposed to choose one? I couldn't, so I bought three different ones. I read the instructions. They are not too difficult, only three steps, but I still have trouble understanding. Eventually, I take one into the bathroom and pee on the stick. I leave the stick in the sink. I have to wait three minutes for the results to develop.

Three minutes. Doesn't sound too long, but it also sounds like an eternity. I turn on the television, but all the channels annoy me. They are too loud and too bright. The shows are too stupid.

I need a drink.

I search the cabinets for my mom's not-so-secret stash. I find a bottle of wine and pour myself a glass. This will calm me down. I put the glass to my lips and take a sip.

Shit!

I spit it all out.

What if I'm pregnant? I can't have a drink while I'm pregnant.

Agh! I scream. I'm not much of a drinker, but I hate how when the craziness of the situation finally calls for a drink, I can't have one.

"That's fucking perfect." I say. I put on the kettle instead. Tea. Soothing, calming tea. It will put me at ease. At least, a little bit.

I listen for the kettle to get louder and louder until it gives off one last puff and turns off once and for all. I take a moment to choose just the right kind of tea bag. Ginger tea is one of my favorites, but before I left I bought another kind of tea, Jasmine green tea with orange. I've yet to try it.

I rip off the foil and place the tea bag into my cup. The timer on my phone goes off. Three minutes are up. The results of the pregnancy test are up, but I can't look at it yet.

That's funny, I smile to myself. For the last hour, I've acted like a crazy person rushing around – running to the car, speeding to the pharmacy, speeding back home – all in an effort to find out if I'm pregnant or not in the shortest amount of time. And now that the test is done, I need more time.

I bring my tea cup to the kitchen table and sit down. I can't look just yet. My whole life is about to change completely, if the result is positive, and I can't bring myself to face that quite yet.

The tea is boiling hot, but I take a sip anyway. I dunk a biscuit into the tea and take a bite.

Well, this would definitely explain why I've been so hungry and lethargic.

When I'm done with my cup of tea, I walk over to the bathroom. "Be brave. Either way, it's going to be okay," I say to myself.

I walk over to the sink and pick up the pregnancy stick.

"You're pregnant."

The words are in blue, and they stand out against the whiteness of the pregnancy test. I thought that I would throw the test down and sob and cry if I saw that I was pregnant. But I don't.

Instead, I feel calm and at peace. I'm not terrified or upset. I'm fine.

Wow, I'm actually fine.

I smile at myself in the mirror.

"I'm pregnant, and I'm fine," I say.

I go into the living room and sit down on the couch. I wait for my head to get flooded with thoughts of incompetence and all sorts of doubts, but nothing comes. My mind is clear. Free. Empty. Happy, perhaps?

CHAPTER 33 - SOPHIA

That night I call the only person I can think of. I haven't spoken to Tara in years. We went to high school together, but after high school she moved a few towns over, and we fell out of touch. From social media, I know that she has been married since we were eighteen and has a ten year-old stepson. Her husband was a teen father, and he now works as a volunteer firefighter while she stays home and takes care of their son.

I don't know what else to do. I pick up the phone and dial her number. I need someone to talk to, and I just hope that she answers.

Two hours later, Tara is sitting across from me in my living room. She's exuberant and red-cheeked and here. Actually here.

"I can't believe you came over so quickly. It has been so many years and still..." I say.

"Yes, of course I'm here for you, honey. I've wanted to reach out to you for so long. I'm happy to be here." She gives me another hug.

I tell her what happened. I tell her I am pregnant and a brief overview of what I've been doing with my life and my situation with Jax. But tonight, I cover the details. She listens carefully, hanging on to each word.

"So, that's pretty much it," I say when I get to the end of the story. "Would you like anything else to eat?"

Tara is much bigger than I am. She was always a heavy girl, but now she's quite large. Despite that, she's beautiful. Her kindness oozes from her, and I wonder how every single person she encounters doesn't fall in love with her.

"No, I'm fine," she says. "So what do you think you want to do? About the baby?"

I shrug. I don't know.

"Either way, you should probably tell Jax."

I nod. I know she's right. "I don't know."

"What don't you know? You don't think he'll take it well?"

I think about that for a moment. "I actually have

no idea how he's going to take it. But shouldn't I know what I want to do before I tell him?"

"Perhaps. But you know, it's not just your decision entirely. Besides, he might be very supportive about either decision you make."

"But what if I don't want to keep it and he does? What then?"

She shrugs. The very thought of that sends chills through my body. Can I really have this baby just for him to raise it? But what if I don't want to have it and he does? Does that give me the right to get rid of it?

"I just don't know. That's why I wanted to call you. You're my oldest friend, even though we haven't been very close recently."

"I'm always here for you. You know that, right?"

I nod. "I do now."

We sit together without saying a word for some time. I don't know what to say or do, but the mere presence of her puts me at ease. Breathing gets a little easier. My jaw doesn't clench so much.

"What about your mom? Did you tell her?" Tara asks.

Oh, crap. My mom. "No, I didn't." I shake my head and tell her what happened with my mom. About her sickness and recovery. About her becoming a completely different person. A person that would take a long time to get to know.

"You shouldn't judge her so harshly, Sophia," Tara says after listening to the whole story. "You don't know what it's like to be on the brink of death like that. It's very difficult and probably terrifying. She's just trying to live her life now. Who knows what kind of regrets she's trying to get past now that she's actually alive."

I never thought of it that way. To me, as it is with probably many people, my mom isn't a whole person with her own desires and hopes and regrets. She's just some reflection of me. It's crazy to say that out loud, but I never thought of my mom out of my own context. She was always my mom. Not Danielle. Not a woman who survived the death of a child and her own battle with cancer. Thinking of her now as Danielle, I see her in a different light.

CHAPTER 34 - SOPHIA

I decided to keep the baby. I'd thought about it for a while, going back and forth for more than a week, talking to Tara on the phone, going through all pros and cons. Then one day, I just woke up and decided to go with my gut. And my gut said to keep it.

After making the decision, I seemed to have come alive. Energy sprouted from somewhere within me, and I no longer spent my days wallowing or laying around on the couch. I went back to the diner and got my job back. Today is Friday, and I am going to start on the following Monday.

When before I could barely muster up the strength to drive to the grocery store and make frozen dinners in the microwave, once I made the decision to keep the baby, I bought nothing but healthy ingredients and started to cook elaborate and nutritious dinners.

I also decided to tell Jax, but not until I get the confirmation from the doctor that I was, indeed, pregnant. That's where I'm headed to now. My appointment is at one in the afternoon, and sitting here at the stoplight, I can't help but think about how different my life has become in the short weeks that all of this has happened.

The phone rings. I answer and put it on speaker.

"So how are you feeling?" Tara asks. We are now talking at least once a day, and often more than a couple of times a day.

"Good. Excited. I'm on my way to the doctor now."

"I'm so happy for you, Sophia."

"I'm going to tell Jax as soon as the doctor confirms it. You wouldn't believe how much energy I suddenly have. I was moping around for weeks, and now I just can't wait to get up in the morning and start the day."

AND THEN...THE world fades to black.

SOME TIME LATER.

"SOPHIA? SOPHIA?" Someone's calling my name. But it sounds very far away like it's at the other end of a long tunnel.

I give up. My eyelids are just too heavy. I can't open them. Not yet.

SOME MORE TIME LATER.

"SOPHIA? SOPHIA?" This time, the words are closer. They are no longer a tunnel away. My eyelids are a little less heavy. I manage to open them. Harsh light floods in, blinding me.

"Sophia? She's opening her eyes! Sophia?"

The voice sounds familiar. The sound of it makes my heart seize up.

"Sophia, please wake up. Please."

I try harder. Someone's rooting for me. Someone very important.

When I finally open my eyes, I see Jax. The concerned look on his face morphs into relief. His eyes are filled with hope.

"J-a-x?" I manage to say. There's something in my mouth. But someone removes it. My mouth is dry. My lips are chapped. I've never been this thirsty.

"It's okay. You're going to be okay."

SOME TIME LATER STILL.

I WAKE and sit up in a hospital bed. I don't know how much time has passed or what day it is. All I know is that Jax is no longer wearing his casts, but is walking around on his own.

"I love you," he says over and over again. "Do you know that? I love you. I should've told you a long time ago, but I was afraid. And I didn't know how to say it."

I stare at him. I don't understand what he's saying. Or why.

Tara's also there. She looks guilty. Happy to see me, but guilty.

"What's wrong?" I ask. And then I remember.

"You were in a car accident. A tractor trailer ran the red light. You're lucky to be alive," Tara says.

And then I remember. It's not just me.

"And my baby…" I ask.

No one says anything. I don't know if Jax knows. But by the look on his face, I suspect that he does.

"What happened to my baby?" I ask. No one wants to say it. It's not good news.

"You lost the baby," Tara finally says. "I'm so sorry."

THE WORLD FADES TO BLACK.

CHAPTER 35 - JAX

Tara is the one who calls and tells me about the accident. I drive to the hospital in a daze. From the tone of her voice, I can tell it is bad. Strangers don't just call other strangers about accidents if things aren't bad.

When I finally get there, I see a girl lying in a hospital bed. She is Sophia, but at the same time, she isn't Sophia. Not my Sophia. Gone is the exuberant, feisty girl who became one of my closest friends over the last few months. Gone is her laughter and her smile. Instead, what remains is some sort of fragile shell of a person she once was.

And then Tara tells me about the pregnancy. About how she was going to keep the baby. My baby. A million thoughts swirl around in my head.

Thoughts that I am ill-equipped to deal with. Thoughts that I have to simply put out of my head just to get through the days.

Sophia lies in an induced coma for three days. We don't know if she is going to live or die. I stay the whole time. When I call O and tell her what happened, she comes to stay with me. She doesn't have to. I asked her not to, but she insists. It's like something is different about her, too.

"I love you. I love you," I say to Sophia when she first opens her eyes. I didn't say it when we were together and lived to regret it. So now that she is finally awake, I am not going to miss my chance.

"I love you," I say to her again this morning. "I want you to know that I always have."

She smiles at me. She knows about the baby but doesn't say anything else about it. We try to focus on today. I try to make her laugh. I read funny stories to her from my phone. I show her funny videos of cats and dogs. Finally, she cracks a smile. A few hours later, she manages a laugh.

MY SISTER HAD WANTED to see her for the last two days. Ever since she woke up. But I didn't want her to. Things between them got so bad and so complicated, I didn't want Sophia to be uncomfortable in any way. But after Sophia finally laughs, I decide to bring it up.

"O is here. She has been here this whole time. For the three days that you were in a coma and the last two days that you were awake."

"Really?" Sophia looks surprised.

"Yes. And she wants to see you."

Sophia shakes her head.

"Please?" I ask again. But Sophia again shakes her head.

"She doesn't want to see you," I say to O, who's waiting outside.

"No, I have to see her."

"You can't."

I'm adamant, firm in my position. "If Sophia doesn't want to see you, then that's it. You can't."

I think she believes me. I think that she accepts Sophia's decision. But I should know better. As soon as I start to walk over to the vending machine to get a cup of some terrible hospital coffee, O marches right into Sophia's room.

"Sophia, I'm so sorry." I hear O say. "I'm so sorry about everything. I was such a bitch to you. I don't know what came over me. But I shouldn't have acted that way."

I come back to the room to pull O out.

"You can't be here," I say. "She doesn't want to see you."

"I know. I'm leaving. I just wanted you to know that. Okay? I feel terrible about all this."

I'm about to drag O out, but Sophia stops me.

"It's okay," she whispers and sits up in her bed. "Go on."

O apologizes in a way I've never seen her apologize before. I've never heard her be so sincere and honest. She talks about how awful she felt after her boyfriend dumped her and she wound up pregnant. She talks about how lost she'd felt and how coming back home was the only place she felt safe. And she talks about how much she hated Sophia for being there.

"I'm sorry, okay." O sits down on the bed next to Sophia. "I was awful. I just wanted to apologize for being so awful and ask you to forgive me."

Sophia takes a moment.

"Okay," she finally nods and smiles. "Okay."

CHAPTER 36 - SOPHIA

I have been back "home" with Jax and O for three weeks. He says that this house is my home, and slowly but surely, I've started to believe him. Did I really have another home? The trailer where I grew up and lived with my mother for all of those years wasn't really a home anymore. Not really. She was gone, traveling around Europe with her new boyfriend. And now that she was basically an entirely different person, the place that we had shared no longer felt like home.

I continued to get better and better every day. The car accident had some residual effects, of course. Goose bumps run up my arms whenever I hear the screeching of tires or the honk of a horn. But otherwise, I was starting to feel like my old self.

"At least you never lost your memory," O keeps saying. She's right. I remember almost everything leading up to the accident and everything after I came out of that coma. What I remember most about her was how shitty she treated me when she first came to live here. But, the funny thing about life is that, just when you think you have something figured out, it changes on you.

"From the way O and I are getting along now, you'd think it was she who fell into a coma." I remember joking with Jax. To say that O is now nice to me is the understatement of the century. She's kind, sweet, accommodating. She's starting to show now, and every day that goes by, every day that the baby grows bigger inside of her, the nicer she seems to get.

"I thought the hormones were supposed to make her worse," Jax says, lying in bed with me one morning.

"Maybe only in the first trimester." I shrug.

It has been three weeks since I left the hospital, and it has been longer than that since we talked about our own baby. The only real casualty of that fateful car crash. I don't know how to bring it up, and I get the feeling that Jax doesn't want to bring it up. Though I love this new O, who has somehow become one of my closest friends, seeing her belly swell does make me sad. I'm excited for her, but I am also devastated for my own child.

Everything about the accident is unfair, but it is out of my control. What I can control is how I react to it. How I allow it to affect my life. At least, that's what I read on some new age self-help site. And when I first read those words, I thought they were the answers that I was seeking. I felt better. Calmer. But now, I realize that everything that has happened to me over the last year has been pretty unfair. It was just the accident that was particularly unfair and bad. But what is there to do? Nothing. I have no control over this. None of this.

It is in this mercurial state that I check my email on my phone. The sun is shining brightly outside, and Jax keeps wanting me to go horseback riding with him, but I can't muster the energy to get out of bed. Now that Jax got me a phone with better cell reception and actual coverage to allow me to go online, I have very little energy to do anything but lie around in bed.

There's an email from Danielle. My heart drops and, at first, I don't dare open it. What the hell does she want? I don't know what my main issue is with my mom, but something about the thought of her makes my whole body tense up. On one hand, I'm happy for her. At least, I want to be. I'm happy that she found someone to spend time with, someone who can afford to take her to Europe. I'm glad that she's living her life to the fullest. After everything that she has been through with losing my sister and getting diagnosed herself and nearly dying in the process, she really deserves to be happy. So why can't I be happy for her? Perhaps, I'm a selfish, self-centered girl who wants her to be unhappy for the rest of her life. No, that can't be it. It's more than that. At least, it's not all that.

I finally get the courage to press 'open' and scan the email. I don't read any of the words carefully enough. I don't linger. I simply move on from line to line. My mom rambles on and on how much she loves Switzerland and Barcelona and Madrid – apparently, they're in Spain now. She asks about how I'm feeling and mentions that she's glad that I have such a wonderful boyfriend to take care of me. Again, she apologizes for not coming to see me in the hospital and mentions that she totally would've if Jax had said that things were turning for the worse.

"I was in a fuckin' coma, Mom! How much worse could things get?" I talk at my phone. I want to toss it across the room, but it's not the phone's problem that I don't want to get this email. I take a break, breathe in and out, before continuing.

"Great news: I'm getting married!" I read the line over and over. It's at the end of the email. I read all the words around it and read it again, but it still doesn't make sense.

"We want to get married in LA when he comes here on business next month. It's not going to be a big wedding, just our closest family and friends. I'll write you more about it later when we get the details figured out. How exciting!"

Getting married? Is my mom kidding? How the hell is she getting married?

I get up and pace around the room. I can't breathe. My chest hurts. I crack my knuckles and wince from the pain. I didn't do it right. Fuck. How is this happening? She doesn't even know this person that she's marrying. They've only known each other a few months. That's not enough time at all.

"Can you believe it?" I ask Jax as soon as he comes into the room. He doesn't know what I'm talking about it. I show him the email. It takes him forever to read it and respond.

And when he finally does, he simply asks, "So what? Isn't this great news?"

I don't even know who this person is standing before me and pretending to be Jax.

"What are you talking about?"

"I don't get it." He shrugs. "Your mom's getting married. She sounds happy. What's wrong with that?"

CHAPTER 37 - SOPHIA

WHEN IT ALL GETS TO BE TOO MUCH…

The way he phrases it puts me off guard. I take a step back. There really shouldn't be anything wrong with it. This would be fine for someone else's mother, but not mine. She's not the type. She worked in a diner almost her whole life. She lived in a trailer park. She doesn't have any prospects. She has fought cancer her whole life. First with her daughter and then with herself. My mom simply does not do this.

"My mom isn't the type," I finally say. "My mom isn't the type of woman who meets a European stranger late in life and has this torrid affair with him. And then marries him."

"I can see that you're very upset about this," Jax

says. "But let me put it this way. Aren't you a lot like her?"

"How so?"

"Well, you grew up in the same trailer park. You had basically the same life minus cancer. And yet you found me. I'm also not a very typical option for someone like you."

Now I'm not sure if he's insulting her or me.

"I didn't really mean it like that," Jax quickly corrects himself. "All I'm trying to say is that you never know what kind of things will happen in life. And you can't just go around trying to live in some sort of box that you put yourself in. Your mom has lived her life in a box for a long time. Maybe this is her way to just try to get out of it."

I nod. Perhaps.

"Besides, it's not like you two have any money."

"So? What does that mean?"

"I mean, it's one thing if you had money or some sort of trust fund or something. Then you'd worry about this guy's intentions with her. But you don't. So that's one thing you don't really have to worry about."

I think about that for a moment. Jax is right. My mom and I do not offer this stranger very much in terms of finances. It is probably his family that is worried about some poor American who he is going to marry. Perhaps, things between them are simpler than I think.

"There you go." Jax smiles at me. "I can tell that I'm starting to make sense to you."

I smile, too. "Maybe you're right. Maybe she is in love."

He wraps his arm around my shoulder. "But what if she doesn't know him enough? I mean, this hasn't been that much time. She only met him a few months ago."

"Even if it's not, even if this is a big mistake. So what? Isn't that what life is about? Giving it all, even if it is a mistake?"

So what, huh? I think to myself. Maybe I need to adopt that attitude as well. So what?

My phone beeps again. Another email. But Jax takes it away from me and presses his lips onto mine.

"What are you doing?" I mumble.

"Nothing," he mumbles back through the kisses. "I want to kiss you."

"Oh, you do, do you?" I say. He presses his body to mine and intertwines his fingers with mine. A rush of excitement courses through my body as he pulls me on top of him. We fall onto a soft feather bed. Jax starts kissing my shoulder and neck. I close my eyes and enjoy the moment.

His tongue is soft and kind and strong when it needs to be, and it has sent me to the heights of ecstasy and the depths of despair.

Beep. Beep.

The sounds break my concentration. I'm not usually the one who's obsessed with my phone. Even out of the two of us, Jax is the one who checks his a lot more. But something is pushing me to look at it. Why? Another email from my mother? Perhaps. It's not like I have a job that sends me emails. Still, I have to answer it.

"Oh, where are you going?" Jax tries to grab me and pull me back into bed. He's only successful in pulling off my button down shirt. "Leave it alone. It's just a phone. Who cares who it is?"

"Let me just look at it for a second, and I'll be right back." I smile. I want to be back in bed with him. I want to kiss him and touch him and take off all his clothes.

I pick up the phone and look at the screen. The new email takes a moment to load. As soon as it loads, I drop the phone. I pray that Jax thinks it's an accident even though it wasn't. I dropped it because of his name.

Ryan.

Ryan?

Ryan!

How the hell did he find me? No, no, no.

"Oh, shit." I get down on my knees. I reach for the phone, but Jax is quicker than I am in my fragile state. My mind is racing, but my body is standing still. I can't make one decision or perform one action. I'm lost and afraid. My frozen hands shake uncontrollably.

"Let me see this," Jax jokes. "What is so important for you to get out of bed and look at? It better be from your mom."

He's smiling and joking, but I can barely crack a smile. My mouth runs completely dry and my lips are chapped.

"Okay, so Danielle says..." His voice trails off. I can't see what he's looking at, but I know it's bad.

"Sophia, who is Ryan?" He turns to me. His voice isn't accusatory or distant. More like curious.

"Um, Ryan..." I say. I don't know where to begin or how to explain. This is my secret. My shame. One that I never planned on sharing with Jax. "No one. Not really," I say.

He stares at me. Then hands me the phone. Reluctantly, I take it.

"Hi, sweetie. I'm coming back to town. Would love to catch up. Love always, Ryan."

I read the email silently. I don't know what to do with myself. His words aren't frightening or scary on the outside, but they cut me to my very core.

"It's no one." I toss the phone aside. "No one important."

"Well, I didn't think so," Jax says. "But then I was just witness to the expression on your face. What's wrong? Who is this guy?"

I shrug. I don't know how to begin to explain.

"And why is he writing 'love always'? Is he your old boyfriend?"

I nod. "Yes, he's just not quite over it."

This part is true. Ryan McPhee is an old boyfriend. He's someone I cared a lot about at one time. But that was such a long time ago, I can't even remember who I was then.

"So, are you going to tell me what's wrong?" Jax asks. He's not letting it go. And the more I resist, the worse it's going to get. And yet, I still can't find the words to explain.

"Seriously, he's nobody. Just some old jerk I have no intention of ever contacting again." I put on a brave face, but it's no longer just brave. I'm acting the role of someone who's not really scared. Someone who is powerful and strong and untouchable. I wrap my arms around his neck and kiss him. We fall into bed together again, and I just hope that the passion in our kisses is enough to erase any memory of Ryan.

CHAPTER 38 - SOPHIA

WHEN HE WON'T STOP...

*O*ver the next couple of days, I got two additional emails from Ryan. They said basically the same thing, but they scared me just as much. Each email made me more and more nervous. Each email made my blood run cold, if not colder than the one before. The second email also came with an apology.

"Listen, I'm sorry for everything that happened. Let's make up. Love always."

The casualness in his tone made me want to rip his eyes out. Who the hell does he think he is? But instead of letting him get a rise out of me, I simply reply.

"Please don't contact me again."

I'd debated whether I should've written that to

Ryan for some time. Each time going back and forth. Changing my mind over and over again. On one hand, it would be good to just ignore him. Completely. Not give him any reply at all. Just pretend that I didn't get the messages. On the other hand, I thought that asking him to stop might evoke some remaining feelings of humanity left within him. Perhaps, if I'd asked him to stop then he might actually comply with my wishes. Eventually, I did write back and spent the next day agonizing over whether this was the right decision or not. And then another day later, I finally decided to send it.

My thumb hovers over the word 'Send.' To send or not to send. That is the question. I press send. And regret the decision almost immediately. My throat closes up. My chest begins to ache. I can't take a full breath of air.

Shit. Shit. Shit.

My mind goes blank. This can't be happening.

"Hey, Sophia." Jax barges into my room. I whip around in the chair and drop the phone. He walks in cautiously and picks up the phone.

"Are you okay? You've been kinda off ever since that email."

I nod. I still don't know how to tell him the truth. I should, but I can't.

"I'm fine." I give him a little peck on the cheek.
He deserves a lot more than that, but I just can't
bring myself to show him any attention. Not since I
got the emails.

"I'm just a little freaked out about my mom's
wedding," I lie. I've almost entirely forgotten how
freaked out I was about her wedding. It scares me,
too, but not like this. Nothing scares me as much
as this.

"It's going to be fine." Jax tries to comfort me. He
puts his arms around me. Kisses me. But I can't
reciprocate. I feel like I can't breathe. Like the world
is closing in around me.

"Are you sure you're okay?" he asks, looking me
straight in the eye. He doesn't believe what I'm
saying. And I don't think that my body language is
any more convincing.

"Please tell me if something's wrong, Sophia.
Things have been off ever since that day. But I get the
feeling that it's not just your mom's impending
nuptials."

"What do you mean? What are you talking
about?" I try to act innocent. My acting is abysmal.
My hands get impossibly cold. I can't even open up
my fists to warm them up.

"I just don't really understand what's wrong with

you. I feel like there's a lot you're not telling me."

"About what? About Ryan?"

Shit. Why did I have to say his name? He probably wasn't even thinking about him.

"Yes, about Ryan." Jax crosses his arms across his chest. "I know you better than you think, Sophia. I know when something's off. You've been walking around in a daze around here for days. It's like you're afraid of him, or something."

I'm terrified, I think. But I don't say a word.

"So, are you?"

"No." I shake my head. "I don't know what you're talking about," I say with a shrug. "Everything's fine. I'm just feeling a little under the weather, that's all."

"But if something is wrong, you'll tell me, right?" Jax asks.

I nod.

"No, you have to promise me. Out loud," he says and waits.

I'm not confident that my voice can manage it without giving me away. I take a deep breath.

"I promise," I say.

CHAPTER 39 - JAX

WHEN I CHECK ON HER...

Sophia doesn't know this, but I check her phone. She had been acting so scared and awkward that I have to find out what else is wrong. I am expecting to see more emails from her mom. But what I find instead makes my heart sink.

Two more emails from that guy Ryan McPhee. Two more emails.

Each email has an apology for what had happened. What?

In each email, he asks Sophia for a chance to see her again. To apologize in person, presumably, but this isn't stated explicitly.

And the worst thing, each email ends with the same "Love Always, Ryan."

What does this mean? Who is this Ryan

McPhee? And why does the mere mention of him make Sophia so uncomfortable? I try to put myself in her shoes. I have ex-girlfriends, too. Some I like more than others. There might be one or two of them who would freak me out if they ever contacted me and wanted to make amends, but I doubt that I would ever react like she has. Like she is reacting. What is her reaction exactly? A shutdown. But not a quick shutdown with a one swoop motion. Instead, it's a slow shutting down like the way people die after a long illness. One organ shuts down at a time.

The only thing I can think to do is to look him up on the internet. I googled him last night and came up with a list eighteen pages long of Ryan McPhees, who all live in California. Of course, I don't even know if he does live in California. That's just an assumption and one that can easily be wrong. What it seems like from the emails is that he doesn't live anywhere near her mom's place, but that's about as narrow as I can get. And that, too, is also an assumption.

O is now as big as a house. I can't tell her this without fearing for my life. She walks briskly, but all of her movements are so exaggerated I sometimes think that she resembles a clown in a fat suit. I'm not really this immature, of course, I know enough not to mention any of this. It's just that I've never seen a pregnant woman before. Not so up close and personal.

Today, she enters the kitchen with both arms full of groceries and fresh flowers.

"Please take these now, NOW!" she yells. I run over and grab everything from her just in time. The groceries are from the farmers market. So they are all packaged in eco-friendly, recyclable paper bags, which are bulky and awkward to carry.

"You think you got enough groceries?" I ask. O has become obsessed with eating cleanly. No frozen dinners. Nothing with MSG, whatever that is. Nothing processed. She even started to make her own hummus.

"I'm going to make a quiche for dinner tonight," she announces with a wide smile. I stare at her. I'm still not used to this new and vastly improved version of O. She cooks and cleans and nests as if there's no tomorrow.

We have yet to talk about her ex. The father of her unborn child. But she has been so friendly, upbeat, and happy ever since Sophia came home from the hospital that I didn't want to break the spell by bringing *him* up. Clearly, she wasn't in the mood to discuss him or she would've brought him up herself, I reason. O is never one to shy away from an uncomfortable topic of conversation.

"A quiche, really?" I ask, furrowing my brows. That sounds complicated.

"Yes, really." She rolls her eyes. I'm sure she knows why I'm surprised. How can I not be? I've never seen my sister bake a thing in her life. Up until a few months ago, I doubted that she even knew what an oven was or how to turn it on.

"You've really come a long way, O," I say. I hope that I sound encouraging rather than sarcastic.

"How so?"

"Well, remember how I got you that 'Microwaving for One' cookbook for your birthday a few years back? And you told me that you tried making something from it and it was too complicated."

O bursts into a laugh. Strong and powerful and unashamed. I'm suddenly reminded of my old sister, the one who was never afraid to laugh too loud or dance as if no one was watching.

"I have come a long way since then, haven't I?"

I nod. "I like this version, though. It's a good version."

She smiles and winks. "Me, too."

"Can I ask you something?" I ask when she starts

to lay out all the ingredients for the quiche. I figure it's as good a time as any.

"Sure, shoot."

"Sophia got these emails from some guy named Ryan."

"What kind of emails?"

I tell her everything. She listens carefully as she chops the spinach. She thinks about it for a moment while whipping the eggs.

"No, I don't believe it's anything, Jax. That girl loves you. I see it in the way she acts around you."

I think about that for a second. She's right. Of course, she's right. And yet, something in the back of my mind gives me pause.

"I know," I finally say. "I know. But I'm just not so sure. What if I'm wrong?"

"You're not wrong."

"Okay." I take a deep breath. I didn't want it to come to this, but I need a second opinion. "Well, that's why I sent them to myself."

"You did what?" O's eyes grow wide.

"She just acted so weirdly. I didn't think anything at first. But then, I wasn't so sure. So I sent them to myself when she was in the shower."

O shakes her head.

"I know, I know. It was a really shitty thing to do, wasn't it?"

"Kind of. You know, if this turns out to be nothing, then she'll really feel like you violated her trust."

"I know." I hang my head. I feel my shoulders sloping down and taking the whole world with them.

I get my phone out and show her the emails. O reads them carefully. I wait, trying to guess her reaction.

"I don't know," she finally says. "This guy, Ryan, sounds desperate, in love maybe. But I still don't think you have anything to worry about."

I try to figure out what's worrying me. I just don't know.

"The thing is that it's not even really him or what he says. It's her reaction. She looked...I don't know, uncertain? Scared? In some instances, petrified even. She was trembling when she got the first one."

"Trembling?"

I try to convey exactly what I saw, experienced, but whatever words I find are not enough. There was a lostness to her. A kind of sorrow.

"Maybe she's just afraid of your reaction to them. Seeing you two together these past few weeks," O smiles, "you two are getting along so well. You're so happy. I just don't think this is anything for you to get jealous over."

O is trying to be reassuring, but I'm not convinced. On one hand, I know she's right, of course. But on the other, I'm not so sure. There are other factors in play. Facts that I'm not aware of. And that makes me worried. We are happy. It's not an act. But the emails, they have to mean something, right? Why else would she react that way?

"How about this?" O puts her hand around my neck. "Why don't you just ask her?"

"Just ask her?"

"Yeah, what's the worst that can happen?"

CHAPTER 40 - JAX

WHEN WE GO HORSEBACK RIDING...

The following day, Sophia is still acting strangely. I've tried to bring the emails up a few times, but the problem is that I'm not supposed to know about the emails. Plural. I'm only supposed to know about one. And I can't very well accuse her of keeping the others away from me without incriminating myself.

But there's something else on my mind as well. Sophia and I haven't had sex since she got Ryan's first email. She's trying to act normal, but it doesn't feel natural. It's like she's forcing herself to be friendly. Or maybe it's just my own feelings being mirrored back to me?

"Want to go horseback riding today?" I ask Sophia, popping into her room after breakfast. I'm not expecting a yes, by any means. I've gone horseback riding multiple times without her, and she has avoided going with me for weeks for a variety of reasons. For one, she's afraid of horses. She can't even let one smell her hand without recoiling. This isn't really a good sign, not according to most horse experts. According to lore, only people who are inauthentic are afraid of horses because horses can spot a fake from a mile away.

Another reason is that she's angry at Sebastian for breaking my legs. They're not all like Sebastian, of course. For one thing, they're not all young stallions. I've reassured her about this multiple times, but she still won't step foot into his part of the barn.

"Sure, that will be great," Sophia says. I look at her, unsure if I heard her correctly.

"What?" I ask. I've forgotten the question.

"Let's go horseback riding." She smiles. I'm not sure if I believe her.

"Really? Why the sudden change of mind?" I ask her when we are already on our way over to the barn.

"Just looks fun," Sophia says. There's a slight hesitation in her voice as if she's trying to cover something up. But I'm not going to let her back out.

"Hey! Hey!" I hear someone yell behind us. I turn around and see O wobbling toward us. It's supposed to be a run, but at this point she's so pregnant that it's not really a run anymore.

"Hey! Wait up!" she yells when we are already standing still near the barn. When she finally reaches us, her beet-red face sparkles in the sun. She grins from ear to ear.

"Are you okay?" Sophia asks. "What's wrong?"

"No, nothing," O says, catching her breath. "Really good news. Just give me a moment."

We wait in anticipation for her to get a handle on her breathing. She seems to be taking her sweet time.

"I just talked to your mom," she finally manages. "She's getting married. Do you know that?"

Sophia's face falls. She looks at the ground. There's a mixture of anger and disappointment building behind her eyes.

Finally, she nods. O doesn't seem to notice a thing. Excitement flows out of her and she loses her breath again.

"I just talked to her and she's really into doing a very small wedding. She was actually thinking of eloping, but then she thought about you and how much she wants you to be there."

"Oh, thanks," Sophia says sarcastically. "I'm glad that she gave her only daughter at least that much thought."

"Anyway." O rolls her eyes. "Danielle and I talked about what she wanted, and she was thinking of going to a courthouse and doing some small dinner in LA. And then I said, why doesn't she just come to our house?"

"Our house?" The prospect of a wedding at our house scares the hell out of me. "No, no, no, O. Don't you remember the disaster that was Mom and Dad's vow renewal ceremony? It took like a year to plan and it occupied the house for nearly a month."

"Hear me out, Jax." O puts her hand up.

"What the hell are you doing?" I can't help but laugh. "Sticking your hand in my face? What is this, the 90s?"

"Okay, sorry. I just need you to hear me out. Sophia! Where are you going?"

I turn around and see that Sophia is already halfway back to the house. I run after her calling her name. O follows slowly behind me.

"Sophia! Wait up!" I grab her arm and spin her around.

"Leave me alone." Sophia's crying. Large, round tears are slowly rolling down her face. Her lips are puffy and the lip gloss that had only a minute ago glistened on them has disappeared.

"Where are you going?"

"What does it matter? Leave me alone!"

"Sophia, please," I try again. But I feel like I'm losing her.

"Leave me alone, Jax! Let go. I don't want to talk about this anymore."

I let her go. O finally catches up.

"Sophia, please. Wait. I didn't tell you everything," O says. Sophia turns on her heel to walk away but then stops.

"And what is it that you left out? How you're going to have this glamorous wedding for my mother and her wealthy fiancé here at the house? And how much fun you two will have planning all the details? And picking out the dress?"

"No." O shakes her head. Sophia doesn't understand. "No, not at all. That's the thing. Your mom doesn't want a big wedding. It's going to be hardly a wedding at all. More like a special occasion dinner. They're just going to say their vows, and then we'll all have dinner. No one's coming besides you and us. And the only reason I think Jax and I are even invited is because we live at this house."

Sophia hesitates. I feel her processing all the information.

"She doesn't want a wedding?" she finally asks.

O shakes her head. "No, not at all."

"Not at all?" I ask. A wave of relief covers me from head to toe.

"I knew you'd be ecstatic about this, too," O says, pointing to me. "He's not one for lavish parties."

CHAPTER 41 - SOPHIA

WHEN WE HAVE A FIGHT...

I can't believe the roller coaster of emotions that I went through when I heard about my mom's wedding. I'd agreed to go horseback riding with Jax because I've reached the end of my rope regarding reasonable excuses. He has become really suspicious of practically everything I do ever since the Ryan emails, and I needed to find a way to reconnect with him. We haven't had sex since I got that first email from Ryan. And that's unacceptable.

Walking over to the barn, I was trembling. Shaking like a leaf on a cool autumn day. I heard somewhere the horses can tell right away if you're not being honest, and I was terrified that my secret from Jax would come to the surface. Then, just when

I was worrying about the whole Ryan debacle, a whole other thing shook my world.

My mom is getting married. She's actually doing it.

And she's coming here. I'm not exactly sure how I feel about this last part. O is excited. She's over the moon to be exact. But me? I don't know.

"Are you okay?" Jax asks. I turn to face him. I'd completely forgotten that he was in the room. How long had I been staring into space like this?

"Yeah." I flash him a quick smile. "Fine."

"Not so sure," he says, picking up his phone.

In the span of only a few weeks, we have managed to become an old married couple. Not sure how all of this took place, but suddenly, there is an ocean between us, even though there are only inches that separate our bodies.

Only a few weeks ago, just lying this close to him would've sent shivers over my whole body. All I would've thought about is how to find just the location for my arm so that I can brush up against him accidentally. But now. Now things are different. My mind is elsewhere. On two things specifically. My mom's impending nuptials and Ryan's disconcerting emails.

"Sophia? What can I do? What's wrong?" He puts

his phone away and faces me.

"I want this to work," he says. I'm covered in cold sweat.

"What do you mean? I want this to work, too. Very much so."

"I'm not so sure." He shrugs. "Things are so different between us now. It's like you're running away from me or something. Every time I see you, you make some excuse to avoid me. To not spend time with me."

"No, no, I don't." I don't know what else to say but deny the truth.

"Yes, yes, you do." He's not letting me get off that easily. "There's something going on that you're not telling me."

I shake my head.

"Why are you lying to me, Sophia? Why?"

"I don't know what you're talking about."

"Really? Really? You're going to go there?" He gets up and takes his phone. I shrug and wait.

"And what about these emails? You got two other emails from Ryan after that first one. He's apologizing. He wants to see you."

The whole world goes silent. I feel like I was punched in my stomach. How does he know about the other emails?

"Are you going through my phone?"

"Yes, I did. I'm sorry about that. But you were acting very weird, Sophia. I had to do something. I had to find out what was wrong."

I can't speak. My mouth is parched and I feel like I'm going to pass out any second now. "I can't believe you went through my phone."

"I'm sorry. I'm really sorry about that. But please tell me what's going on with Ryan. At first, I thought it was nothing. Just some ex. But your behavior after you got the emails just got stranger and stranger. Now I know that something's going on."

I can't say a word. I feel like I'm choking. I also want to choke him.

"No," I finally manage. "Nothing's going on."

It's not true. A part of me is screaming on the inside to tell him. Tell him the truth. It's not as bad as he's imagining it to be, but my fear is not letting me. I'm too scared to tell the truth. So all I can do is lie. And get mad.

"There's nothing going on, Jax. Not with Ryan and me. But I can't believe you went through my phone. Are you that fuckin' insecure? Are you that much of a coward?"

I'm riling myself up to make all of this his fault. It's not right, but blaming him is all I can do in this situation. There's a look of disappointment in his eyes. Quickly, it turns into anger.

"I thought you were better than this, Sophia. I thought that we had something real."

"We do. But we can't continue to have it without you trusting me."

"I do trust you," he whispers. "At least, I did until right now. I know that something is going on. With you and Ryan. Otherwise, you wouldn't react like this."

"You don't know shit," I say and turn away from him. Just tell him the truth. The truth. It's not that bad. It will stop him from thinking all these bad things about you. About you and Ryan. I try to find the words, but nothing comes out.

"There is no me and Ryan. He's some ex. That's it," I finally manage to utter.

"Why is he writing you? What does he want?"

I can't even imagine. I can't let my mind go there. Shivers run up my spine, and I start to shake. Jax doesn't know what he's talking about. What he's asking me to say.

"What is he apologizing for, Sophia? What happened between you two?" he asks carefully. He can probably sense my anxiousness. The depths of which he will hopefully never know.

"Nothing really." I shrug. But I have to offer him more than that. "Okay, we dated. For a bit. Not long. And then I broke up with him. That's it."

I pray that that's enough information. But it's not.

"So what is he apologizing for?"

I need to offer him more. Tell him the truth, I say to myself over and over again while Jax waits patiently.

"He just didn't take it very well, that's it," I finally say. I can't look Jax in the eye. I feel like he can sense the truth just by looking at me. When we finally do make eye contact, I realize that he can't. His expression is completely blank. Like one of those that Buddhist monks have when they reach enlightenment. I saw a documentary on them recently on Netflix, and it clearly left an impression.

"Is that all?" Jax asks quietly.

"Yes." I nod. Please leave this alone. Please. Please. Pretty please.

"You're full of shit, Sophia. You know that?"

His words hit me so hard, they knock the breath out of me.

"It's true," I whisper.

"No. No, it's not. You know that. And I know that," he says and walks away.

When he reaches the door, I start after him.

"Jax, please."

"We have nothing else to talk about, Sophia. Unless you want to tell me the truth."

"This is the truth." I start to sob. Please believe me.

"No, it's not." He shakes his head and walks out.

Big fat tears start to roll down my face. I'm a coward. I'm a freak. Why couldn't I just tell him the truth? I love this man. I did nothing wrong. And yet, something kept me silent.

Of course, I know perfectly well what it was that kept me silent.

Pain. Shame.

To admit what happened was to make it true again. It was to contaminate this house with all that darkness and hopelessness. No, I couldn't do that. I can't do that.

But was that worth this? Worth Jax thinking that Ryan and I were anything at all? Worth Jax having doubts about me and how much I love him?

Love. It's nice to hear this word. I love him, too. I've known I loved him for a long time now. And until the emails, I was pretty sure that he loved me, too. Shit. Shit. Shit. How could I screw this up so badly? I bury my head in my knees and cry until all sense of time disappears.

CHAPTER 42 - SOPHIA

One day passed. And then another. And then another five. Jax and I still didn't speak. He avoided me in the hallways and ate dinner and lunch at different times from me. O still spoke to me, thankfully, and she was sweet and kind and a friend that I really needed.

"I think I'm going to leave soon," I tell O at dinner on the sixth day of our silence.

"What? No!"

"Yes." I nod. "After the wedding."

The wedding is in two days. My mom is arriving tomorrow morning. I tried to get out of it. I tried to get her to move it to somewhere else. But O interfered. She said that she didn't care that Jax and I were no longer together or were having drama.

Danielle was her friend, and the wedding was not getting cancelled just because things got a little tense.

"No, you can't leave!"

"I have to. I don't think Jax and I are together anymore. He won't say a word to me. And I just can't stay here like this. I don't really know what I'm doing here."

"But you're my friend, too. Please stay. Stay until after the birth, at least."

I think about it for a moment. She's due in two months, but I don't think I can manage here for that long.

"I don't know, O. I'd love to. But this thing with Jax and me is serious. He won't say a word to me. I don't think I can stay here for two more months like that."

"Are you sure you can't work it out?"

O knows about Ryan. At least, as much as Jax does. And that's enough. I can't share any more than that.

I nod. "I don't know what he wants from me. He doesn't believe me when I tell him the truth. What else can I do?"

O shrugs. She feels my pain. I can tell by the hurt expression on her face. The problem is that I know what else I can do. I can tell him the truth. The real truth. The one that he feels is somewhere below the surface of all our conversations. The only problem is that I'm a coward, and I can't bring myself to tell him any of it. I can't bring myself to say any of it out loud.

And the worst part of all this is that I'm willing to give up the best thing that ever happened to me because I'm such a coward. It makes me sick to my stomach.

My mom arrives the following morning. She is as radiant as I've ever seen her. Her hair shines in the sunlight, and her skin has a beautiful glow to it. Her eyes are wide, and she's wearing fake eyelashes that make them look triple their normal size. And there's something else. I can't quite put my finger on it.

"Hello darlings." She hugs me and then O. "Oh, what a beautiful place you have here! It seems to get more gorgeous every time I visit."

When she embraces O, I finally realize what it is that adds to her beauty. Her lips. They aren't pursed from tension and anxiety anymore. Instead, they are calm and relaxed. Glowing just like the rest of her.

"Here, let me introduce you to my darling husband to be. Luke!"

A distinguished man with a few gray hairs on the sides extends his hand. I'm about to shake it, but instead he brings it up to his lips and kisses the back of my hand.

"It's a pleasure to meet you, Sophia," Luke says with a slight French accent. His words are soothing.

I watch my mom introduce Luke to O, Mr. Whitewater, and eventually Jax, who all respond warmly to his calm demeanor. After all the introductions are made, Luke takes my mother's hand and tells everyone what a pleasure it is to meet her friends.

There's a genuine goodness to his way of being in the world. He hugs my mother when he doesn't have to, as if he is drawn to her by some invisible magnet. Not long ago, Jax and I had this same way of being. It's called being in love. Even before O takes my mom and me upstairs for the dress fittings and the men head to the other part of the house to try on tuxedos, I know that what my mom and Luke have is real.

"So what do you think?" Mom takes my arm on our way up the stairs.

"I like him," I say. "He seems to really love you."

"Oh, sweetie." She wraps her arms around my shoulders. A wave of relief sweeps over her face. It's like she has been holding her breath, and now she can let it out.

It makes me happy that I can provide this sense of relief for my mom. And it makes me even happier that, at this moment, I'm not lying. I'm telling the truth. It feels good. So good, that for a brief moment, I consider telling Jax the truth.

"C'mon, let's go." O takes my hand. "Danielle, I can't wait to see you try on the dresses that I picked out for you."

My mom stares at her dumbfounded. "I thought I would just wear something I already have. I have this little yellow summer dress that Luke got me in Paris."

The smile nearly vanishes from O's face, but she is quick to recover.

"Yes, of course. Whatever you'd like. But since the dresses are already upstairs, maybe you'd like to take a look?" O says with a mischievous look in her eye.

I'm sure that that look has served O very well over the years and has had quite an effect on many men.

My mom's eyes light up. She has always loved shopping. Even when we had absolutely no money, she would go to Target or Ross and browse the aisles. Inevitably, she would come home with some crazy marked down pair of jeans or a beautiful top, which she only paid five dollars for.

"When did you have time to get dresses?" I ask on our way up the stairs.

"Oh, you don't think I was just lying around here all day doing nothing, did you? I've been hard at work planning this little shindig ever since I heard of it."

I shake my head and smile. I'm glad that there are women like O in the world. Women who get immense pleasure from planning and organizing events. I'm glad, mainly, for selfish reasons. Because I don't have that event planning gene, and if the world was made up of people like me, then civilization would be doomed.

CHAPTER 43 - SOPHIA

T wait on the couch in O's room for my mom to try on her first dress. O is in the walk-in closet with her because, according to O, "trying on wedding dresses is a three or four woman job, but we'll manage."

I offered to help out, but both of them insisted that I stay put.

Finally, my mom comes out. My jaw drops. That's not an exaggeration. It actually drops open, as if I'm in one of those old school cartoons.

The woman before me is tall and elegant and looks like she's ten years younger than my mom actually is.

"So? What do you think?" my mom asks,

smoothing the large taffeta skirt of the wedding dress with her hands.

"Beautiful," I manage to say. Tears come to my eyes, but I try to hold them off. I can't believe that this is my mother standing before me. I've never seen her this beautiful and radiant. This effervescent.

"Yes, you do look lovely, Danielle," O cuts in. "But there's another one that I think might be a little bit more you."

"Another one?" I ask.

"Yes, how many dresses do you think I got exactly? Just one? What kind of fitting would this be?" O tosses her hair and rolls her eyes. I smile.

When my mom disappears into the dressing room, O turns to me.

"You really like that dress?"

I nod.

"I think the skirt is a little full. It makes her look a little bit like a recently groomed poodle."

I nod. I don't know what to say. That was the most extravagant thing I've ever seen in real life, and I'm in awe of its grandeur.

Before I get the chance to gather my thoughts, my mom comes out again. This time, she's wearing a long gown that hugs her hips and makes her look as if she were six feet tall.

"This is an A-line dress," O explains. "It accentuates your figure a lot more, giving you a very, very nice shape. What do you think, Danielle?"

This time, it is my mom who has tears in her eyes. She wipes them off with the back of her hand.

"I'm sorry. So sorry, I didn't want to just disintegrate into a puddle, but it's beautiful."

"Well, this is it then," O says, decidedly.

"This is it? Aren't there more dresses to try on?" I ask.

"You don't know the first thing about shopping for a wedding dress. Do you, Sophia?" O asks.

"No, why?"

"Well, if you did, then you'd know that the first dress that makes the bride-to-be cry is the dress. No ifs, ands, or buts. This isn't a science, darling. This is an art. And the first dress that produces that reaction is the one!"

We both turn to my mom. She's staring at herself in the mirror. She's never looked lovelier, and she knows it. Tears are streaming down her face. Tears of happiness and joy. The kind I can't remember the last time I've seen. The kind that I really wish my little sister was here for.

"And for us, the bridesmaids, I got us these lavender dresses." They are cut to the knee with built-in cups and thin straps going over the shoulder. The material is the lightest thing I've ever felt. This must be what it feels like to be a butterfly, I think to myself when I look at myself in the dress in the mirror.

"The color really complements Sophia's skin tone, don't you think, Danielle?" O asks.

"You're breathtaking," my mom says, choking up again.

We start to do our own makeup, but O remains in charge.

"First, you've got to put on the primer," she instructs. "It's like painting a house. Would you ever paint a wall without putting on primer first?"

Mom and I just stare at her. I don't actually know since I've never painted a wall or a house. I have put on foundation before, but apparently without primer, and that's all wrong.

"All of these years of applying makeup and I've been doing it all wrong," Mom jokes.

O sprays on our foundation then blends it with a wide brush. Fake eyelashes are next. The glue frightens me, so I just close my eyes and pray that O doesn't glue them shut. She applies the eyeliner and the eyeshadow next and follows that up by filling in my eyebrows.

At first, I try to protest and do my own makeup. But once the fake eyelashes come out, I just give up and give in. So does Mom.

When O's finally done, I look at myself in the mirror and don't recognize the beautiful woman staring back at me.

By four o'clock in the afternoon, we are all ready. Just in time for the ceremony. O leads the way, taking us to the garden. My mom looks like a movie star. She moves as if she were floating on air.

The wedding will take place in the garden's gazebo. When we walk into the garden, Mr. Whitewater is standing at the head with a small book before him. Luke is right next to him on the right, and Jax is next to him. Luke looks like all fiancés do in movies, nervous, lonely, and incredibly handsome.

I follow O down the aisle. In the end, I turn to Jax. He's radiant. The tux accentuates every hard line of his body. It looks as if it were made to just be worn by him in this world.

"Doesn't Jax look handsome?" O whispers.

"Very," I say. I try to meet his eyes, but he purposely avoids mine.

When the music starts, I turn away from him and look at my mother. She walks down the aisle slowly and majestically, as if she was born to do this. At this moment, she is no longer my mother. She's Danielle. A woman on the verge of starting her new life with the love of her life, and I can't be any happier for her than I already am.

When she gets closer, I see that the most beautiful thing that she's wearing is the smile on her face. The last time I saw her this happy was when my little sister was still alive. And that was many, many years ago.

The wedding passes in no time. Mr. Whitewater reads from the Bible and asks the bride and groom if they promise to care for each other in sickness and in health, for better and for worse. They say their "I do's" and lock lips.

"Okay, let's all head out to the foyer for cocktails," O says as we walk down the aisle following the happy couple. Throughout the ceremony, I tried to meet eyes with Jax, but he had successfully evaded me until we were supposed to lock arms and walk back down the aisle. Finally, I thought. This will be my opportunity to at least touch him. No matter how chaste.

But he didn't give me his arm. When I reached

for it, he recoiled and walked slightly ahead of me. It took a lot of courage for me to reach out to him. I hope he knows that. I also know what he would say if I'd said that out loud. "Why don't you just get the courage to tell me the truth?"

I will. Later this evening. I will tell you everything, I promise myself.

CHAPTER 44 - SOPHIA

When I get to the foyer, I head straight to the bar.

"What would you like?" the bartender asks. He doesn't look familiar. He was probably just hired just for the occasion.

"Martini. Dry, please."

I should've started drinking a long time ago. At least, way ahead of the ceremony.

"Here you go, madam." He hands me the drink.

"Excuse me, sir. You can't be here. This is a private party." I hear someone say behind me.

"Don't worry, this won't take long. Only a few minutes."

I drop my glass to the floor. That voice is all too familiar and frightening.

Time stops. I turn around. Everyone's still mingling, talking, and for a brief moment, Ryan and I are the only ones in the room.

"Hi, sweetie." He takes a few steps forward and is suddenly right next to me. He's breathing on the back of my neck. Suffocating me. I want to move my feet and run, but I'm bound to the floor. Frozen from fear.

Out of the corner of my eye, I see that he's carrying a handgun.

"Wow, you're even more beautiful than I remember," Ryan says, brushing his hand against mine.

I shudder and recoil from his touch.

His wide black eyes are devilish and sinister. Arrogant. I can't believe that I was ever drawn to them.

"Can I help you?" Jax comes closer. I don't know if he knows about the gun. I want to scream for him to go away and stay away. This man is armed and dangerous. But I remain still and barely breathing.

"Yes, you can actually. I'm here to pick up Sophia," Ryan says, tossing his head back. His shoulders are square with Jax's. He's challenging him.

"Pick her up for what?" Jax asks.

"Not for anything. Just pick her up. She's coming with me."

"I'm sorry, who are you?" Jax asks. "Do you know this man, Sophia?"

"Tell him, Bree," Ryan says.

But tell him what? The truth that I should've told him a long time ago. I can't do it now as much as I couldn't do it before.

"Okay, then. If she won't do it, let me do it. My name's Ryan McPhee. And Sophia and I are together. She's the love of my life. She got lost for a little bit, but now she's back."

Jax stares at him. And then turns to me.

Finally, I summon courage from someplace deep within me that I didn't even know existed. I'm shaking. But my words are steadfast.

"We are not together, Ryan. I have a restraining order against you. Or did you forget that?"

Jax gets it immediately.

"You have to leave, Ryan. This is a private party."

"Oh, yes, I know. But I'm not leaving without Sophia," he says and pulls out his handgun. The whole room grows quiet. It gets so quiet I can hear my mom's pulse from across the room.

Ryan grabs my hand, shaking me out of a daze. "Let's go, Sophia."

"Ryan." Jax steps forward. Ryan is too fast for him. "Another step forward and I'll shoot you. You better stay back now, you hear?"

Everyone stops in their tracks. Out of the corner of my eye, I see O's terrified face.

"Let's go, Sophia." Ryan wraps his cold, strong hands around my waist and pushes me forward.

A thousand thoughts rush through my mind. I can run, but then he'll shoot me. Someone could get hurt. I'm not sure everyone in the room realizes just how crazy he is. Just how out of control.

Outside, the clouds that have been gathering ever since the ceremony finished suddenly break out into thunder. A few aggressive flashes of lightning follow, and all of the lights go out. My mom screams. Ryan pulls me closer. I can't see a thing anymore. The whole room is a blur. It's pitch black, and I have no idea where Ryan is pulling me.

A few moments later, my eyes adjust to the darkness. Then, from the distance I see him. I want to yell out to him to stop, to get away, but I don't want to alarm Ryan, who has yet to see him.

With one swift motion, Jax knocks the gun out of Ryan's hand and punches him. Ryan falls to the floor, but he doesn't let go of my hand, and I tumble onto the floor along with him. Jax looks

around for the gun, but Ryan is quick. He grabs
him at the ankles. Jax falls to the floor. Thump.
Ryan's back on his feet. He's holding the gun over
Jax's head.

"No!" I scream out. My voice can't stop a bullet.
Jax moans. He's been shot!

Rage boils within me. The fireplace is right next
to me. I see the metal poker Mr. Whitewater used to
adjust the wood on the flame. I grab it, put it behind
my back, and turn to face Ryan.

"Oh, you think you're so brave defending Sophia
like that? What, you think you're some sort of hero?"

Ryan's talking to Jax, who's writhing in pain on
the floor. He doesn't see me. This is my only chance.
I don't think, don't give a thought. I simply act.

I run straight for him, poker extended. It goes
through his chest. Blood spurts out of his mouth. I
step back to keep it from touching me.

"Sophia." Ryan shakes his head. "Sophia."

Those two words will haunt me forever. Ryan's
legs give out, and he drops to the floor.

"You're going to be okay, Jax. You're going to be
okay." I grab Jax and cradle his head with my body.
He's still breathing, but each breath is laborious. He
has been shot in the stomach. I hear O calling the
police and feel everyone circling the two of us. I feel

them here, but at this moment, we're alone. No one else exists, but us.

Jax opens his mouth and tries to say something.

"It's okay. You're going to be okay. You don't have to say anything," I say. Hot tears run down my face, and I pray that I'm right. But Jax keeps trying. Eventually, he manages to form the words.

"I...love...you."

CHAPTER 45 - SOPHIA

*J*ax, O, and I often talk about that fateful day, the day my mother got married. O had her baby while Jax was still recovering at the hospital from the gunshot to his abdomen. He spent four days in the hospital recovering. I spent another two weeks telling him everything about Ryan and I. Everything that I should've told him earlier. He was my boyfriend for a year, but he got a little clingy. So I decided to break up with him. At first, I thought he took it alright, but he said that he wanted to be friends. And continued to contact me. When I told him that we could no longer be friends, he got angry. Hit me. Pushed me down. I tried to call the cops, but he smashed my phone. When he finally left, I went to the police station and got a restraining order. He was told to stay away, but he didn't. I saw him cruising past my house. He came to the café and sat in the parking lot until someone told him to leave. I called the cops. They enforced the restraining order, told him to stay away, but he kept breaking it. And each time that I saw him, I got more and more afraid.

Then I came to Jax's house. This was the one place where I felt incredibly safe. Ryan couldn't reach me here. He didn't know where I was, nor did anyone else. I stopped hearing from him. Months passed and I thought that he had moved on with his life. Then I got that first email.

My whole life was turned upside down. I started to panic. Fear ate me up inside. I was terrified. I couldn't think of anything but him. The only thing that kept me going was that I really believed that he didn't know where to find me. And then he did.

I didn't know how he found out about this place, but then I got a call from my mom. Apparently, her trailer had a break-in and some documents were missing. One of them was the letter from Grayson, Inc. and another from Jax about repaying the debt, along with the letter was his return address.

"He must've just come here on a hunch," Jax says

when we talk about it again. Jax's home now, but still a little weak from the medication.

"Yeah, that must be it," I agree.

"I still can't believe you did that," he says.

"Did what?"

"Killed him like that. That took a lot of courage, Sophia."

"I'm just sorry that I didn't do it earlier before he shot you." I put my hand in his. "I knew how dangerous he was, and I just let it go. Let the scenario play out."

"No, you didn't." Jax smiles and kisses the top of my head. "You didn't know he was going to shoot me. He was crazy. You couldn't have predicted any of this."

I try to believe him.

"Hey, I've been meaning to ask you something. I'm thinking of taking that job in LA working for my father's company. After I get a little better. What do you think?"

"I think that would be so exciting. Yes, definitely. A nice change of pace. You need that."

I'm happy for him, but another small part of me is a little sad. What would that mean for us then?

"Well, I can only do it on one condition, though." Jax flashes his mischievous smile.

"What's that?"

"You have to come with me. Will you?"

I look at him. I can't believe what I'm hearing.

"What would I do there?" I ask.

"Anything you want. It will be a new start for us. What do you think? Please say yes."

I think about it for less than a second. "Yes! Yes!" I wrap my arms around his neck and kiss him. "Of course, yes!"

Then something occurs to me.

"But only under one condition," I say, pulling away from him. "We go horseback riding first. After you get a little better, that is."

"You want to go horseback riding?" he asks. "I thought you were afraid?"

"I am." I smile. "Well, no. That's not entirely true. I'm a little apprehensive, but I'm not afraid anymore."

Jax pulls me closer to him and kisses me.

"You've got yourself a deal," he whispers through the kisses.

———

THANK YOU FOR READING DEBT. If you enjoyed

Sophia and Jax's story, I know you will LOVE Everly and Easton's in **HOUSE OF YORK.**

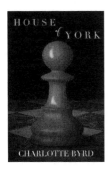

A date with a cute guy turns into my worst nightmare. **Taken and imprisoned, I become a captive.**

Easton Bay, **a dangerous billionaire**, is supposed to be my enemy, but **he risks everything to protect me.** He is my beacon of light in this place of darkness.

I take a deep breath.

It's my turn to be shown.

What happens when **his protection is no longer enough?**

One-Click HOUSE OF YORK Now!

———

Start reading **HOUSE of YORK Now...**

Prologue - Easton

They are not supposed to be here. They are innocent and polite and sweet. Some of them may even be kind.

They think that they are here of their own free will.

They think that it's a game.

They think that everything is going to be okay.

I know the truth.

They are not here by accident. They were all carefully chosen.

Selected.

Identified.

Vetted.

Some are here because they are gorgeous, others because they will be good at bearing children. A few are lost souls who no one will ever look for.

But some, well, they are here because of their ability to fight.

Propensity to fight.

Willingness to fight.

Not everyone wants a fighter. Not everyone wants someone to resist their every move.

But some of them do. And these are the ones who will pay the most. And to find a girl who is both beautiful and a fighter? Well, that's everything, isn't it?

Of course, there will be the ones who fail. Most will fail at least once, but some will fail for good.

We call this game a competition to keep them pacified. Calm. Quiet.

But they had all lost their freedom a long time before they ever stepped foot on the island of York.

All but one will lose their lives.

Chapter 1 - Everly

Freedom is difficult to describe when you have it.

You go through life bogged down by life's little problems. You go to work at a job you don't particularly like.

You get paid way too little.

Thirty-four thousand dollars a year.

Your rent and monthly expenses are way too high.

Fifteen-hundred in rent and another three-hundred in student loan payments plus utilities. Of course, there's the myriad of other little but not inconsequential expenses.

The occasional lunch out.

Happy hour.

A movie once in a while.

Is this what it means to be an adult? I guess so.

After I graduated with my undergraduate degree in Psychology, I decided to work for a few years to save some money before going on to graduate school for my doctorate.

Of course, I wanted to work in the field. The only problem was that the only job I was qualified to do with just a bachelor's degree was to answer phones at a marriage therapist's office.

I scheduled appointments and dealt with the insurance companies. The job wasn't anything I ever wanted to do and I hated it.

I would sit in the freezer of an office with the zipper of my dress pants digging into my stomach, and I would feel sorry for myself. College was hard, but it was nothing in comparison to the grind of everyday life. School was broken up into semesters, and semesters into weeks, and weeks into classes and assignments. Even if a class was unbearable, as some requirements were, at least I knew when it would come to an end.

I can still remember the contempt that I felt for my job and my life, in general. Days became weeks and then months and years and everything in my life stayed the same. Clients called. Appointments were scheduled. Lunch was eaten. Money was made. Bills were paid.

But looking back now, trapped in this God-forsaken place, I would give anything to be there again.

To have that kind of freedom again.

"Number 19," a loud deep voice is piped in on the loud speaker. "It's your turn."

My heart sinks and I take a deep breath.

"I don't have all day," she says loudly.

I know what to do and I do it quickly. I pull off my tank top and take off my pajama bottoms. When the door opens, I'm completely nude. She looks me up and down.

I'm used to their glares. I don't know her name, I know her simply as C. There are twenty-six guards here. All called by different letters of the alphabet.

"Let's go," she says, leading me to the end of the hallway.

The ground is cold and wet under my bare feet. I'm ushered into a large shower room. Five others are there as well. We exchange knowing glances, but none of us dare to say a word.

We have exactly two minutes to wash our hair and bodies. After that, the water turns off automatically and the guards throw us a small hand towel to dry ourselves.

It wasn't that long ago when I worked at an office all day hating my job.

It wasn't that long ago that I thought that I didn't have any freedom.

Now, I know better.

Now, I know what real imprisonment is like.

Now, I know that the life that I hated so much

before is one that I would do anything to get back to now.

After drying myself off, C leads me back to my cell. The walk back is even colder than before, but I appreciate being given the opportunity to clean myself.

"E will be in shortly," C says. "It's your turn to be shown."

My throat clenches up in fear.

To. Be. Shown.

What does that mean?

Chapter 2 - Everly

Being shown.

I've heard whispers about this, but none of the prisoners really know what's going to happen. The guards? They know. Of course, they know, but they aren't talking.

When C leaves, I put my pajamas back on and sit down on the bed. I wrap my hands around my knees, resting my head on top.

I wait.

A few minutes later, E comes in. Her hair is cut short, blunt at the edges, right by her chin. Her eyes are severe, without an inkling of compassion. Her skin is pale. Her bright red lips stand in stark contrast to the gray monotone uniform that all the guards down here wear.

Besides the bright red lips, she is not wearing a smudge of any other makeup.

She lays a garment bag and a big black makeup box on my bed.

"Strip," she says, sternly.

I do as she says. I know better than to resist. Once I'm completely nude, she looks me up and down. She brings her hand to my chest and bounces my left breast up and down, examining it for... something. I don't know what.

"Lie down on your back and open your legs."

I want to punch her. Kick her. Smash her in the face. But I remember what happened. Besides, I can't escape. The door locks automatically, and the only way out is through her fingerprints. Even if I could get out into the hallway, I wouldn't know where to go. And I can't very well drag a body with me to open the other doors.

I lie down on the bed as she says. I spread my legs.

She leans over me and again examines me.

"Stay just like that," she says and brings over her toolbox. My heart jumps into my throat, anticipating what she is about to do to me.

But I calm down a bit when I see her pull out a waxing kit. She warms the wax and carefully applies it to me using a wooden applicator stick.

A moment later, she puts on a strip of cloth and rips out my hair by the roots.

"Ouch!" I moan from the pain.

"Be quiet," she dismisses me.

The next strip she applies, I bite my tongue and keep quiet.

I've only been waxed once before and I ran out of there before the woman could finish. It was just too painful. But today, I don't have a choice.

She applies the hot strips and peels them off with expert precision. A few minutes later, I'm completely bald on top.

"Get on your knees."

"Why?"

"Do it."

I flip over.

"Stick your butt in the air and spread your legs."

I take a deep breath as she applies the hot wax to one of my ass cheeks. When she pulls the strip off, I can't help but yell out.

"Be quiet."

Trying to stay quiet as she finishes, I bury my face in the blanket and muffle my cries.

"Flip over."

"Is it over?"

She pushes me back to my back.

Then she spreads me wide open, exposing every last bit of me.

"Does it look like it's over?" she asks, pointing to the little hairs.

"You're taking all the hair?"

"Every last strand."

As soon as she wipes the hot wax inside of me, I realize that this is going to hurt way worse than any of the strips before. I grab onto the blankets with my hands and hold my breath.

"You're done. Get dressed, you big baby," E says. "Wait, before you do, lift up your arms."

I do as she says. She examines my armpits and then runs her eyes down my body, looking for stray hairs.

"Here," she says, handing me a razor and a bottle of liquid soap. "Go shave yourself."

I walk over to the small sink in the corner of my cell and do as she says. I run my hands down my legs and ask for permission to shave them. She nods. When I'm done, I let her examine me again. Finally, she gives me a nod of approval.

————

AFTER WASHING and drying her hands, she opens her makeup box. The box is so large that it has wheels like a suitcase. She gets out a big spotlight and shines it in my face. There is no mirror here, so I cannot see what she is doing as she starts to apply foundation to my face. All I see are the tools. Foundation brush. Concealer brush. Eyeshadow primer. Eyeshadow brush. Highlighter. After a few minutes, I lose track of everything that she's doing.

"So...how did you get this job?" I ask. Partly out of curiosity and partly out of boredom.

I haven't talked to anyone in days and life gets tedious that way.

But E ignores me.

"You're just not going to answer me?" I ask. She gives me a little shrug. Progress.

"Are you not allowed to talk?" I ask.

"Of course, I am," she says. Apparently, I have insulted her.

"So, why don't you answer me?"

She shrugs again.

"I applied for it."

"You applied for it?"

"Did I stutter?" she asks.

Now, it's my turn to shrug.

"So...you don't live here?" I ask.

I don't really know where here is, but I hope that she can help me figure it out.

"I just work here. I live on the mainland."

Wow. There's that word.

Mainland.

How long have I been here? I'm not sure exactly. But in all that time, I didn't realize that we were on an island.

Do you know what happens here? I want to ask. Do you know that we are all prisoners? You must. Of course, you do.

I want to ask, but I don't know who I'm talking to. She's a stranger. And just because she's a woman, doesn't mean that she is necessarily on my side. She is an employee, after all.

So, I decide to ask something else instead.

"So, what does E stand for?"

"It's just a letter."

"You don't have a regular name?"

"Not here."

"Why?"

"No one here has names. Privacy reasons."

I look straight into her eyes. Is she trying to tell

me something? Reach out? Or is she just stating the facts?

"My name is Everly," I say. I need to make a connection, any way I can.

"No." E shakes her head. "Your name is Number 19. And you will never mention Everly again, if you know what's good for you."

It sounds like a threat, but it's not. More like sound advice from someone who has a little sympathy for me. At least, I hope so.

If she won't tell me anything about herself or this place, then maybe she will tell me something about what is about to happen.

"Why are you here?" I ask. "Why are you doing my makeup? Dressing me up?"

"Because that's my job."

"But what's it for?"

"You are going to be shown."

"What does that mean?"

"There will be a competition. A contest with judges. Only, it won't look like a contest. Everyone will want to be there. It's a privilege just to be chosen. You will all live in a big house together. Play. Have fun. But every few days, someone will leave."

The way she says the word 'leave' sends shivers through my body.

"What do you mean by leave?"

"There will only be one winner. And the winner will get to leave with her life."

"And...go home?"

"No." E shakes her head. "You will never go home. You will be his."

"Whose?"

"I've already said too much."

"That doesn't exactly sound like a contest you'd want to win," I say after a moment.

"It's not. But it's better than the alternative."

Can't wait to read more? **One-Click HOUSE OF YORK Now!**

———

SIGN UP for my **newsletter** to find out when I have new books!

You can also join my Facebook group, **Charlotte Byrd's Steamy Reads**, for exclusive giveaways and sneak peaks of future books.

I appreciate you sharing my books and telling your friends about them. Reviews help readers find my books! Please leave a review on your favorite site.

BLACK EDGE Series Reading Order

We don't belong together.

I should have never seen him again after our first night together. But I crave him.

I'm addicted to him. He is my dark pleasure.

Mr. Black is Aiden. Aiden is Mr. Black. Two sides of the same person.

Aiden is kind and sweet. **Mr. Black is demanding and rule-oriented.**

When he invites me back to his yacht, I can't say no.

Another auction. Another bid.

I'm supposed to be his. But then everything goes wrong....

1-Click Black Rules Now!

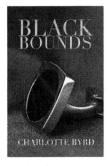

I don't belong with her.

Born into darkness, life made me a cynic incapable of love.

But then Ellie waltzed in. Innocent, optimistic, kind.

She's the opposite of what I deserve.

I bought her, but she she stole my heart.

Now my business is going up in flames.

I have only one chance to make it right.

That's where it happens...something I can never take back.

I don't cheat on her. There's no one else.

It's worse than that. Much worse.

Can we survive this?

1-Click BLACK BOUNDS Now!

They can take everything from me, but they can't take her.

Mr. Black is coming back. With a vengeance.

"I need you to sign a contract."

"What kind of contract?"

"A contract that will make you mine."

This time she's going to do everything...

1-Click BLACK CONTRACT Now!

———

Is this the end of us?

I found a woman I can't live without.

We've been through so much. We've had our set backs. But our love is stronger than ever.

We are survivors.

But when they take her from me at the altar, right before she is to become my wife, everything breaks.

I will do anything to free her. I will do anything to make her mine for good.

But is that enough? And what if it's not?

1-Click BLACK LIMIT Now!

––––––––

Debt Series (can be read in any order)

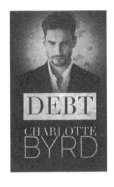

I owe him a debt. A big one.

A **dark and dangerous** stranger paid for my mother's cancer treatment, saving her life.

Now I owe him. But I can't pay it back with money, not that I even have any.

He wants only one thing: Me.

His for one year.

Will I walk away in one piece?

1-Click DEBT Now!

DEBT

OFFER

UNKNOWN

WEALTH

ABOUT CHARLOTTE BYRD

Charlotte Byrd is the bestselling author of many contemporary romance novels. She lives in Southern California with her husband, son, and a crazy toy Australian Shepherd. She loves books, hot weather and crystal blue waters.

Write her here:

charlotte@charlotte-byrd.com

Check out her books here:

www.charlotte-byrd.com

Connect with her here:

www.facebook.com/charlottebyrdbooks

Instagram: @charlottebyrdbooks

Twitter: @ByrdAuthor

Facebook Group: Charlotte Byrd's Steamy Reads

Newsletter

COPYRIGHT

96786370R00205

Made in the USA
San Bernardino, CA
20 November 2018